WITCHES PROTECTION PROGRAM

MICHAEL OKON

WFP
WORDFIRE PRESS

QUOTES

"Badges and broomsticks collide in Witches Protection Program, *a fast-paced, lighthearted piece of crime fiction with a supernatural twist ... With its lively characters, quickly moving plot, and amusing dialogue,* Witches Protection Program *is a great summer choice, ideal for beach or poolside reading, and with elements of romance, action, crime, and fantasy, there's a little something for everyone to enjoy."*

—Pallas Gates McCorquodale, *Foreword Reviews*

"... mixes predictable elements—corporate intrigue, sexy witches, cat familiars, car chases, family secrets, and steampunk weaponry—into an enjoyable story."

—*Publishers Weekly*

"Wes is a fascinating protagonist ... The short, action-laden novel speeds past nuances from developing characters' relationships...but does leave room for a couple of surprises. The story's case

is more or less wrapped up by the end, with a lingering impression that this could be the first of many to come ... Cleverly offbeat, often cheeky, and loads of fun."

—*Kirkus Review*

"Witches Protection Program *is a fun and quick read, and the out-of-the-norm narrative choices make the novel feel like something wonderfully subversive.*"

—*IndieReader*

"Witches Protection Program *is a unique gem, one that's fast-paced with twists, action, and fun characters.*"

—Five Star Review, Liz Konkel, *Readers' Favorite*

"Witches Protection Program *will hook you if not for the action, then the romance and if not for the romance, then the sheer humor, what with its funny dialogue.*"

—Liezl Ruiz, *NetGalley* Reviewer

"Loved this book ... The characters were complex and the dialogue witty. For this book was just plain fun!"

—Carmen Blankenship, *NetGalley* Reviewer

"Memorable and snarky characters, witchy temper tantrums, magical potions, and crazy weaponry abounds."

—Alyssa Schneyman (Educator), *NetGalley* Reviewer

Witches Protection Program

by Michael Okon

Copyright © 2019 NYLA Blvd., Inc.

EBook ISBN: 978-1-61475-995-9
Trade Paperback ISBN: 978-1-61475-994-2
Hardcover ISBN: 978-1-61475-996-6

Cover design by Michael Mastermaker
Cover artwork images by Michael Mastermaker
Kevin J. Anderson, Art Director

Published by
WordFire Press, LLC
PO Box 1840
Monument CO 80132

Kevin J. Anderson & Rebecca Moesta, Publishers

WordFire Press eBook Edition 2019
WordFire Press Trade Paperback Edition 2019
WordFire Press Hardcover Edition 2019

Printed in the USA

Join our WordFire Press Readers Group for
sneak previews, updates, new projects, and giveaways.
Sign up at wordfirepress.com

🏵 Created with Vellum

DEDICATION

Alexander, Hallie, Cayla, and Zachary

Individual commitment to a group effort—that is what makes a team work, a company work, a society work, a civilization work.

—*Vince Lombardi*

There is a fine line between good and evil. It's called perspective.

—*Bernadette Pendragon*

DISCLAIMER

All characters appearing in this work are fictitious. Any resemblance to real persons or witches, living or dead, is purely coincidental.

PROLOGUE

W es Rockville stared bleakly out the dirt-encrusted window into the overcast day. Muffled horns could be heard through the glass. The late-afternoon sun peeked through the tall buildings, painting the streets of Manhattan with touches of gold. He squinted, his broad face crinkling. The bruise on his jaw still pained him, reminding him of his failure. The purple mark had faded over the past three weeks, but he felt the ache deep in his bones. He scrubbed his head. His wiry blond hair sprang to attention with its military cut. Close-shaven on the sides, the jarhead he stubbornly groomed failed, the wavy curls softening the top of his well-shaped head. He tried to make out the billboard across the way, but in his state of mind, the words appeared like a jumbled puzzle, and he didn't have the patience to put them in order.

Harris rushed in without looking at him. His white shirt was wrinkled, and he had sweat rings under his armpits. His bald head reflected the dull lighting. His deep-set eyes were shaded by iron-gray eyebrows that grew comically outward like a ledge. The older man threw his files with disgust onto the cluttered desk, his deep voice growling, "Gone!"

Blue eyes met blue eyes. Wes looked down before his superior continued, his large shoulders hunching in despair. His six-foot-three frame slid low in the seat. "Three years at the state police level."

"Do we have to do this?" Wes mumbled.

"Quiet!" Harris ordered. "You passed all written tests."

"Your point is?" Wes responded sulkily.

"Is that a whine, Rockville? As I was saying, you were cherry-picked for this department. The youngest recruit. I personally vouched for you." Harris leaned forward, his hairy knuckles pressed on the messy stacks of reports on the desk. "It was too soon. I should have left you in the office, but I wanted to avoid putting you where there was excessive paperwork. It's that reading thing; it always holds you back."

"That was disclosed on my application," Wes said coldly. "It's not an issue, sir. I have mastered my disability."

"That may be true, but I feel that I rushed you. This is an elite agency. Only the best are recruited," Harris said, more to himself than to the younger man.

"Are you saying that I don't measure up with the rest of your team?" Wes asked.

"You put me in a terrible position. My own reputation has been brought under scrutiny."

"I'm sorry," Wes said, his voice low.

"You're sorry!" Harris yelled, the purple vein bulging on his pale forehead. Wes stared at it with fascination. "See something interesting? Look at my face. Look at me, Wesley!" Harris was seething.

Wes gazed up.

"You couldn't transport one little old lady," said Harris.

Wes sank lower into the chair, his eyes downcast. "I don't know what happened."

"You don't know what happened? I'll tell you what happened!" A bubble of saliva gathered at the corner of Harris's mouth and exploded off his face as he shouted, "We said don't look her in the eyes!"

"I didn't. I mean, I might have, but—"

"But nothing. You're a disgrace. Your sister is the most distinguished prosecutor in New York City." Harris fell back into his leather chair, his voice losing steam. He pulled an eight-by-ten picture from the side of his desk and pointed to a handsome blond man beaming in a family picture. "Your brother is Head of Counterterrorism." He placed the photo carefully back in its place. Sighing, he rubbed his face. "We're in a goddamn building named for your grandfather."

"I know, Dad."

"Don't 'I know, Dad' me." He held out a large, square hand. "You have placed my ass on the line with your incompetence! Don't expect any special treatment."

"I'm not expecting to be treated any differently than anybody else." Wes bit back the rest of his response. It would be nice not to be picked on because of his circumstances, either.

"You know, I tolerated the episode with the goat."

Wes fought the grin that tugged at his lips.

"Oh, you think that's funny? Your mother didn't think so."

"Getting him into the dorm was a lot harder than getting him out."

Harris shook his head. "This never happened with your brother."

Wes looked away, the smile fading from his face. *Here it comes,* he thought. The comparisons with Andrew. Good old Andy, boy wonder. Top of his class, unbeatable athlete; no matter how many hours he worked, he never needed a shave. Every hair was always in place; his teeth were so white, they gleamed in the dark. Resentment filled Wes's gut as his face heated with shame. In truth, Andrew never competed with him; he didn't have to. All he had to do was show up. Wes had given up trying to meet Andy's bar years ago. The only one who seemed to understand was Wes's mother. She fostered peace in the house, refusing to allow her husband's tough love to intimidate Wes. His father must have been thinking the same thing because Wes heard him mutter, "She always coddled you. Never let you grow up."

"Wes," his father sighed yet again. He looked up to find the older man studying him intently.

"That's not true," Wes said, defending both himself and his mother.

"Hand me your badge," he said softly. He meant business.

"Aw, come on …" The words froze on his lips when he saw the ice in his father's eyes. In complete silence, Wes dejectedly handed his father the badge he had worked hard to earn. He had made it to this special arm of the police that had been founded by his grandfather over fifty years ago—his lifelong dream. It was an undercover branch of a federal division created to do jobs that local law enforcement couldn't handle. Words clogged his throat; his jaw ticked in sync with that of his father. He swallowed, biting back the choking sensation of disbelief.

"You disappointed me, your family, and the entire force," Harris sputtered. "I knew you weren't ready. I shouldn't have sent you into the field."

"Can't you cut me some slack? It was my first assignment. There has to be a learning curve," Wes said reasonably.

"No excuses. Learning curve, my behind. With your background, this should have been a walk in the park." Harris paused, his jaw grinding. "There's no room for that kind of bull in what we do. The only way you're going to survive this debacle is by embracing it."

"I'm not being fired?" Wes asked, hope filling his chest.

"Nope." His father sat silently, his chair turned toward the fading daylight.

Wes gritted his teeth with impatience. If he wasn't being fired, what was happening? He looked at the collection of photos on the wall and cabinet behind his father. Pictures of his sister, Lauren, at a podium at her graduation, the valedictorian of Yale, then being sworn in to the bar. His brother, with his unit in Iraq, or maybe it was Afghanistan; another of him surfing at Phuket Beach and climbing some mountain in Tibet. He focused on his own graduation picture, a small one from his school in Potsdam on a tiny corner of the wall. He glanced at the family photo. His eyes found the young boy in the picture, standing beside his slight mother, pushed into the corner by his larger-than-life father, his brother's hulking muscles casting him into the shade. They were all brilliant. All of them had the ability to excel at everything they did—that is, except for him. Everything took him longer, from learning to ride a bicycle to reading a book. They didn't understand that the words were jumbled. He had to slowly put them in the right order before he could proceed. In fourth grade, Mr. Wayne had armed him with a trick so that with a little extra concentration, he could work things out with no one the wiser. His parents knew, of course. It didn't matter; he was expected to perform, so he worked longer with a driven intensity to succeed. He studied hard to pass; he spent hours at the gym to be able to master every physical test. Many times, others grumbled that his name earned him his grades at the academy, but Wes knew it was the result of working his butt off.

His father's harsh voice interrupted his musings. "You are being reassigned."

"I don't want to be reassigned." Wes stood, pacing the room. "This was my dream. Give me another chance, Dad."

"Believe me, son. This hurts me more than it hurts you."

Yeah, sure, Wes thought. *Why do they always say that?* This couldn't be happening; he was twenty-five and had spent his entire life training for this job. "This is ridiculous! What, are you gonna send me to my room without dinner?"

"You have left me no choice. If I don't do something, the commissioner will bring me up on report," his father said, his eyes boring into Wes's. Harris scribbled a number and then held out a scrap of paper to Wes. "I'm sending you to DUMBO."

Wes laughed. "Like in the circus?"

His father sat back. "This isn't funny. Down under the Manhattan Bridge overpass. In Brooklyn. Memorize the address and phone number, then burn it. Oh, and ask for Alastair. Alastair Verne."

Wes stared at the paper, the faint handwriting swimming before his eyes. "Give me one more chance."

"This *is* your only chance. Blow this, and you're completely out. Not even your mother will be able to help you."

Head down, Wes didn't see his father's blue eyes soften. Harris cleared his throat. "Remember what I said, Wes. Memorize it and burn it. Alastair's waiting for you."

CHAPTER ONE

W es took the subway to Brooklyn, his stomach reminding him that he had missed both lunch and dinner. It was late, and the streets were deserted. His shoes slapped the pavement as he checked the buildings for the address. He searched the block, noting the numbers skipped the address he'd memorized. Panic welled in his chest, and he wondered if he had reversed the numbers with his scrambled brain. *Thirty-four-oh-five, then oh-six, then oh-nine. What happened to oh-seven and oh-eight?* Squeezing his eyes, he racked his mind to recreate the address. Nothing came back but the phone number. Dragging out his cell, he punched the digits, cursing when a recording came on. He was too late. He should have cabbed it. The office was closed.

"What? What, what?" he said. A truck passed, its noisy exhaust drowning out the message. Wes ambled to a darkened corner of the street, pressing the phone to his ear to make sure he heard the message correctly. He stared absently at the setting sun that washed the sky to a faint pink. The light wind ruffled his jacket, sending a chill down his spine. It was an unfriendly street; there was not a pedestrian, baby carriage, or even a delivery bicycle in sight. The policeman in Wes scoured the facade of the brick buildings, looking for a hint of life. There was not even a chirping bird. The sound of cars racing over the bridge created a wind-tunnel effect, so the whole place had an unearthly air.

"The number you've called is currently out of service." Dammit, he'd messed up. He blew air through his lips in a rush. "Please leave a message after the beep."

Closing his eyes wearily, he repeated the number again, then looked back at his phone, the glare painting his face blue. The sun disappeared, bathing the entire street in gloomy shadows. Wes shivered in the cold. *Wait a minute.* He paused. *What number that's out of service takes messages?* He redialed the number. Wes anticipated the beep and held the phone close to his mouth. He said softly, "Alastair? This is Wes."

His phone buzzed with an interrupting incoming call. Swiping his finger, he heard a woman's voice say, "Rockville?"

"Yeah," he confirmed.

"Look to the basement. To the left of thirty-four-oh-six. See the green light?"

A pinpoint of light about the size of an eraser blinked twice. "Come on, Rockville. You're late, and I want to go home."

Tentatively, he headed down the grimy steps, a buzzer sounding as he turned the ancient handle of the door. He stood silently, his eyes adjusting to the bright light after the dim stair-well. There was an ocean of cubicles that seemed to stretch for a mile. The subtle sound of phones ringing became a steady thrum. An older woman with a lopsided bun and half-moon, bifocals greeted him. Friendly eyes looked at him above the lenses.

"You're Harris Rockville's kid." She had a smoker's voice, gravelly, and enough hair on her chin to qualify for a beard. She pulled a pen from her messy hair, noted something on her clipboard, and cracked her gum. Wes looked up, his surprise making her grin. "Yeah, it's shocking, right? You never expected to see such a state-of-the-art office in this dump." She laughed. "You better make time. Alastair's waiting for you, and he don't wait for nobody. My name's Bathsheba, by the way."

"Bathsheba, right," Wes said absently as he took in his surroundings.

Dozens of people were there working. The hum of voices droned into white noise. Television screens with grids and charts hung overhead. Wes noticed they were maps of cities with dots indicating tracking of some kind.

"Follow me, kid." She led him down a gray hallway with mulberry-colored carpet, plusher than anything he'd ever seen in a governmental office. The place had to be a city block wide, with corridors branching off to other conduits. Here and there, a doorway opened. Wes saw that many were filled with groups of people sitting at polished conference tables. Some rooms were dark, with shades drawn, the light of a presentation on screens peeking through the slats of the blinds. Staff walked through the hallways, nodding to each other. Some were in pairs. All had a badge hanging on a chain or attached to a pocket. He squinted, but he couldn't make out the impression on the shield, forget about attempting to read it. He shrugged; while it looked official, it was unfamiliar. For a person who grew up with an entire family in law enforcement, he found it odd that he'd never seen it before.

"What is this place?" he asked.

"This is where the magic happens," she told him cryptically.

She opened the door, whispering, "Prepare to be amazed." Then, with a giant pop of her gum, she disappeared.

"Where …?" Wes turned, looking for the woman, but couldn't see her anywhere. "Where is …?"

"Oh, she's gone. Come in already," a male voice ordered impatiently.

Wes spun to the speaker, his eyes settling on a small man seated at a glass desk. He was in a stylish gray suit but wore a black turtleneck, which made him look like some odd, eccentric leftover from the beatnik generation. He was older than Wes's father; Wes guessed he was somewhere north of sixty, with the thickening middle of a sedentary life, a tanned complexion, and silver hair. His chubby face sported a neatly trimmed goatee. Wes wondered where his beret might be. The man studied Wes with interested black eyes that glowed with merriment.

"What kind of department is this?"

"Mr. Wesley Paul Rockville. Son of Harris and Melinda, brother to Lauren and Andrew. Tough act to follow. Runt of the litter?"

Wes bristled, wondering where this pint-size dude got off calling him a runt. At six-foot-three, he was hardly considered small. "I fail to see what this has to do with my reassignment," he said icily.

The older man ignored him. "The young gun who had his free will sucked right out of him."

"No one took my free will!" Wes shouted, his face hot.

"I think Miss Genevieve Fox did a pretty nice number on you."

"What are you talking about?"

Alastair cocked his head, a smile playing on his lips.

"I don't think this is funny, um … Alastair. I'm getting out of here." Wes had had enough. He was pissed and hungry.

"Sit down, Agent Rockville. It's time you learned about your new assignment."

Wes stood, the muscle in his jaw ticking, his teeth grinding. He took a deep breath, plopping onto the leather chair opposite the strange-looking man. "This doesn't look like any government agency I've ever seen." He relaxed, allowing his legs to twist the chair so he moved with nervous energy.

Alastair sat quietly, observing Wes's bouncing leg. Wes forced himself to stop moving.

"We are quite secret, I assure you. What did your father tell you?"

Wes's lips compressed in a mutinous line.

"I asked you a question," the older man said quietly.

"He told me I was being reassigned here and if it doesn't work out then I'm finished."

Alastair nodded. He sat back, his short, stubby fingers idly rolling an expensive pen. Wes gazed at the large, opaque window, staring at his bored reflection.

"Your former position was in a branch of the police founded by your grandfather. Only the best are selected."

"I know my family history," Wes said rudely. "Are you implying that I was unqualified?"

Alastair ignored Wes's response. "We are a sort of extension of that unit. A black op, if you will."

"You're delusional," Wes said, leaning back in his chair and lacing his fingers over his flat stomach. He shook his head slowly. "There's no such thing as black ops with policing organizations. Besides, if I wanted to be in black ops, I would have joined the army."

"I wouldn't be so sure of that," Alastair said. "What do you know about witches?"

Wes turned to look at him, his face puzzled. "Witches? You mean like Halloween?"

Alastair leaned forward, his face intent. "No." He shook his head. "I'm talking about broom-flying, cauldron-stirring, soul-sucking, mean-spirited witches who wreak havoc on society."

"Is this a joke?" Wes was not amused. "Because if my brother put you up to this, I don't think it's funny."

"Miss Fox was a witch—a bad one, category eight, ten being the worst." Wes made a rude noise, but the older man continued as if he hadn't heard it. "She looked you right in the eye and disintegrated your free will."

Wes stood. "This is ridiculous. She hypnotized me and every man on that bus."

Alastair shook his head. "Is that what they told you?"

He pointed his pen into Wes's face, and Wes felt the intensity of a light hurting his eyes. He turned his head. "Cut that out."

"You want something to drink?" Alistair opened his bottom drawer, taking out a silver flask. Wes refused. "Take a sip. You're going to need it."

Wes grudgingly took the container, sipping carefully at the contents. It was Frangelico, a hazelnut liqueur, sweet and nutty and strangely relaxing. It hit his empty stomach with the force of a bazooka. "We're a bit new to be drinking buddies."

Alastair laughed as he took a healthy swig. "Oh, rest assured. We are not drinking buddies, but you're going to need this by the time we're through. Some of what you are going to learn is a bit ... hard to swallow."

Alastair rose and came around the desk. He perched his hip on the corner as if he were sharing a cozy story. The room had a strange intimacy, closed off from the rest of the world. "The program you are so fortunate to be a part of was established many years ago to protect witches."

"You're crazy, dude." Wes smiled lazily.

"Not so crazy. They've been around for years, living underground and hiding their abilities. But that is just the tip of the iceberg. The history of witches and our country goes way back. Please pay attention to the monitor." Alastair gestured to the far wall. Wes noticed he aimed a remote at the blank space.

Images flickered on a screen Wes hadn't noticed was there. It filled the room with cinema-quality actors, and Wes stretched out his long legs, getting comfortable.

It was in black-and-white, grainy documentary style. The words *Salem, Massachusetts, 1692* identified the time period. Fields of corn and small cottages: clearly New England during colonial times. Villagers milled about primitive streets. Wes admired the realism of the set. The camera focused on an old crone scrabbling through packed-dirt streets. She was short; her basket rested on her ample hips, and her face was hidden by a mob cap. A man's gravelly voice spoke as the scene changed to a one-room farmhouse, where a woman bent over a boy who lay sweating on a cot.

"I knew we shouldn't'a let Goody Prudence in with her potions."

"We had no choice, husband. Daniel's fever still rises," his wife told him, wiping a tear from her gaunt cheeks. "I know not what to do."

The man stood before a huge hearth, his foot resting on a fender. He stabbed at the logs, his face angry. "The boy doesn't improve even with her potions! I never should have listened to ye." He bit hard on his pipe, his dark eyes squinting in the dim light of the cottage. "Aye, she's evil, that one. John Darby told me so, he did. Aye, her with her potions. They be poison, and she done kilt the boy."

The woman gripped her stomach, howling with misery. "Never say so, husband. I trusted Goody Prudence." She paused, looking forlornly at her sick child, her face twisted with anguish. "Mayhaps he'll improve."

"His breathing worsens. Why did ye bring her?"

"She birthed our boy. Her herbs have worked before."

"Kilt John Darby's cow," the man said, his eyes boring into hers. "Fought over the north pasture. Don't ye remember, Bess? The magistrate ruled for Darby. She gave him the evil eye then."

Bess considered her husband's words and then slowly said, "Aye, I remember. She be staring at me fierce. Did ye see the mark on her chin?" she added maliciously.

"The cow died. Now our boy." He rested his head on his arms and leaned on the wooden mantle of the fireplace. "She be a witch," he said quietly.

The room dissolved to a street scene. The older woman was harried by a group of men holding lanterns and pikes. Wes sighed, bored. A familiar voice that sounded like an actress he had seen in a movie the night before narrated more of the story. *She must be slumming,* Wes thought with a snicker.

"People believed that many women had powers that could render others sick, ruin harvests, even kill livestock. It was a ghastly time, and nobody was safe from these accusations."

"It's that Jennifer An—" Wes said with astonishment. "You know, what's her name? The actress from that show everybody loves? What kind of budget do you guys have?"

"Shh," Alastair admonished him.

The saga continued with the old lady running through dense foliage, ripping her clothing. Dogs barked in the distance.

"You have any popcorn here?" Wes asked. Alastair ignored him.

"Anyone could be branded a witch," the voice-over went on. "Once they were accused, they lost everything, from their farms to their families, and finally—"

Wes winced as the old woman was captured and beaten. This was rather graphic for a training film. He squirmed uncomfortably.

"—their lives," the narrator finished. The screen filled with scuffed and worn boots dangling from a tree.

"Okay, I've seen enough." Wes stifled a yawn; he hated history. His stomach rumbled.

"No, you haven't. We can't move on until you fully understand what we are doing here," Alastair informed him.

A courtroom was the next scene. Two groups of women were standing before a high bench. An imperious judge, clad in black with a white-scrolled wig, stared down his long nose at them. As the camera panned the room, Wes realized that half the women looked clean and attractive, while the other group was scruffy and unkempt.

That actress's voice continued. Maybe he was wrong, but her voice was so familiar. He tried to place her. Maybe it was one of those celebrity chefs. He was sure he recognized the voice from somewhere.

"Pay attention, Wes," Alastair whispered.

"The problems escalated as harvests failed, and squabbles broke out in the villages. Both petty jealousies and long-standing feuds were the catalysts to involve the law. Soon the sisterhood of witches turned on one another."

Wes perked up as the pretty group of women flirted with the judge.

"Looks like a potential catfight," Wes murmured.

"Are you taking notes? There's a test afterward … I'm kidding, Wes. The information will all come together. Relax."

One woman loosened her collar; another tucked an errant hair under her cap. Licking her lips, she coyly said, "It wasn't me, good sir. Goody Abigail"—she pointed a slender finger at a slovenly woman on the other side of the room— "she put ideas in my head, she did. She made me bark like a dog."

The room erupted. The judge slammed down his gavel.

"Quiet! Quiet! Go on, mistress. What else did Goody Abigail do?"

"She spake in tongues!" another shouted. "She be a witch."

"Look at her, Judge," the first female said, her voice seductive. "She looketh like a witch." She walked over, circling the old woman, sniffing. "She has an odor of brimstone and sulfur. I saw her—" She spun to face the judge, her voice loud. "She danced with the devil! Naked!"

Shouts overwhelmed the judge's cries for order. Now Wes watched raptly as the frumpy witches were led to the gallows. The voice-over continued with more sad details.

"The accusations caused a great schism. Witches split into two factions: The Davinas and the Willa. Both groups continued to practice their brands of magic even though they disappeared into the fabric of society. Davinas mastered medicine and healing. You may have known one as a teacher or a nurse. They used their powers for the good of mankind. The Willa went dark—very dark—embracing the nefarious arts and anything that thwarted goodness. They hid their intentions and were shunned by society but used circumstances to make mayhem. For close to a century, no one could identify them, and no one was safe, not the Davinas, and not us."

Wes recognized Mount Vernon, President George Washington's home. He had been there on a field trip in the fourth grade. The plantation bustled with activity; and the Potomac sparkled with the sun's rays. The camera swooped through the main entrance, finding the First Family enjoying domestic bliss. Martha Washington, her dress spread around her like spilled lace, sat in a dainty chair, stitching a piece of fabric while the general was sprawled in his armchair, reading.

In the distance, cackling filled the air. Mrs. Washington dropped her embroidery, her face ashen. She rose and slowly walked to the window. "General, do you not hear it?" she whispered.

"Stay away from the window, madam. They are far off," he said sharply.

The echoes of ghostly voices screaming, "Martha, Martha, Martha!" filled the room.

"Nay, husband. They draw near." She turned, her hand near her face in alarm, "George, you must do something."

The narrator continued. "It wasn't until this land became my land that the government decided to create an organization to protect women at risk. The Davina Doctrine went against everything that the Willas stood for. Even though they ran the risk of persecution, the Davinas chose to work with law enforcement to expose the evil deeds of their rival sisterhood. President George Washington established secret legislation under Title VI of the Control Act of 1792. The law was enacted to protect the good witches who exposed the evil deeds of their sisterhood."

The screen dimmed, leaving only a chair in the center of a stage on which sat a blonde-haired woman, the top of her head lit by a single spotlight. Wes was right; it was the actress he'd suspected. She had a hit sitcom and two Emmys, and there was some recent Oscar talk about her last movie.

"Yes, there are witches living among us. Some are women who believe in using their powers to protect love and life. And then there are others who use their powers for all the wrong reasons."

The camera came to rest on her beautiful face. She winked saucily as she placed a black, pointed witch's hat on her head. "Welcome to the Witches Protection Program."

Alastair smiled broadly. "I love that part."

"That was Jennifer Anis—"

Alastair went on as if Wes hadn't spoken. "Operations have been kept secret for over two hundred years. Davina witches in the program are given twenty-four-hour security while in a high-threat environment. Money for housing, schooling, essentials, and medical care is provided. As of today, over sixty-three thousand witches have been protected. In the entire history of our fine program, we've never had a breach of security in which a protected witch was harmed."

Wes laughed, shaking his handsome head. "I don't believe in witches, sir."

"By the time you're done, oh, I promise, you'll believe in witches. No one grows up thinking they're going to be protecting a person who uses magic and spells to get what they want." Alastair rounded his desk to take his seat again. "But when someone needs to be protected, does it matter who they are?"

Wes looked back mutely, unable to think of an answer. He was wondering why someone with an Emmy and a possible Oscar was doing public service films.

Alastair continued. "Believe it or not, we need witches in society." This caught Wes's wandering attention. Alastair smiled at the younger man's expression of disbelief. "When a witch changes from being a belief to being a force of nature, that's when a witch goes bad. My job"—he paused—"*our* job—is to protect the good ones and investigate the bad ones."

"Yeah, sure. And what about the trolls and pixies?"

Alastair shrugged indifferently. "Oh, they never give us any trouble."

"I was kidding."

"I know, Wes. I'm not."

"Is my father aware of all this?"

"Indeed he is. We finish what his division can't. He has assigned you here because if you can succeed here, you'll succeed anywhere."

"Is that your motto?" Wes asked with a chuckle.

WITCHES PROTECTION PROGRAM

"No. It's actually 'Defenders of the Craft.'"

Before Wes could respond, Alastair walked over to a blank wall and waved his hand. A portion opened with a hiss. Wes joined him, whistling at the array of weapons attached to designated spots. They weren't any kind of firepower he'd ever seen before.

"They're real?"

"You bet." Alastair reached in and took out a lethal-looking automatic that had a huge bulb at the end of its semi-translucent muzzle. It was covered with bronze gauges and metal gears mounted atop an antique grip.

"What kind of gun is that?"

"It's a Steampunk Vaporizer. It's good for long distances."

"I prefer my Glock." Wes pulled his gun out from inside his jacket.

Alastair clicked his tongue. "That toy will be shoved so far up your ass, you'll be praying for it not to fire. Catch." He threw the weapon to Wes, who caught it expertly. He hefted the surprisingly light gun. Wes aimed it at the wall, looking through the crosshairs of the scope.

Alastair nodded. "It's locked and loaded, so be careful."

"I bet you were a big Dungeons and Dragons fan," Wes said, taking a bead on an imaginary target.

Alastair, ignoring him, held up a slim, plastic-looking rectangle about the size of a candy bar.

"TV remote?"

Alastair smiled, revealing a line of gleaming white teeth. Wes noticed his eyes were black and amused. "A Darrow Trance Lifter. They stopped making them for a while. This one's old but works like a charm. Ha." He laughed at his joke.

Wes laid down the rifle, examining the device. "How do you use this?"

"Point and shoot. Don't overthink it."

He handed him an ancient-looking handgun similar to a Colt. It was shaped like a revolver with a cylinder attached and bubbled with green liquid. The grip was made from a metal Wes had never seen before. Despite its size, it was surprisingly light in his hand. All these weapons felt like toys.

"Lastly, this one should be on you at all times." Alastair tossed him a polished disk. "Open it."

Wes caught it and carefully touched the lever, watching with fascination as it opened like a clamshell. He turned it over, looking for buttons or holes for a laser. He was expecting something ... more. Confusion showed on his face.

"It's a mirror. You'll know when to use it," Alastair informed him.

"Come on. This is bullshit. None of this is real."

"I assure you, Wes, it's all very real. These are the only known tools and weapons to stop a witch," he told him as he walked to his desk. Opening a drawer, he took out a roll of duct tape, which he pitched to Wes. Wes caught it, shrugged, and put it next to the gun.

"It's the little things that will save your life," Alastair told him. Reaching down, he shuffled through a few folders, found what he was looking for, and held it up for Wes. "Your first assignment."

"Okay, so let's say for a minute that this is all legit—witches exist."

"Along with trolls and pixies," Alastair added, his face utterly serious.

"Right, yeah, witches, trolls, and pixies. Where have they been for the last three hundred years?"

Alastair leaned back in his oversized chair. "Right under your nose. Have you ever felt compelled to buy a product you didn't need? Stopped for a meal when you weren't hungry? Asked out a girl you'd never noticed before? They've been around for years, living and working alongside of us. The Willas ran underground when women got the right to vote at the turn of the last century. But they pop up to stir the pot every now and then, make life dangerous for the Davinas. That's where we come in. We protect and relocate the good witches. Keeps the peace."

"Pretty big operation for something that happens every now and then," Wes told him.

"Cuban Missile Crisis, the mortgage meltdown, Hurricane Katrina. Are they big enough?"

"Hurricane Katrina?" Wes asked with disbelief.

"I told you, when a witch changes from being a belief to a—"

"Force of nature, that's when they become bad," Wes finished.

"Good. You were listening. Something big is going on. There's been a lot of chatter for months. This all could be connected in some way." He held up the folder again. "As I said, your first assignment."

Wes took the folder ungraciously and snapped it open to look at its contents. It took him a while to organize the wording in his mind so he could understand it. "I can't believe this. I'm not doing it."

"Okay, then your choice is to hand in your resignation and explore the employment opportunities at Frankie's Fried Fish on the corner. You won't have to work hard at disguising your reading problem there."

Wes threw down the folder. "Who told you about that? Nobody knows, and I am able to read just as well as the next guy. It takes me a little longer, is all."

"I know. I timed you. So, being that I have a boss to answer to and that boss wants me to take you to meet Junie 'Bags' Meadows of the Meadows Witch family, I strongly suggest you pick up the folder and get to work." Alastair grabbed his trench coat and an umbrella from a stand. "Come on," he called from the door. "It's time to earn your paycheck."

"Yeah, sure." Wes started for the door. Alastair stared pointedly at the duct tape abandoned on the chair. Wes rolled his eyes as he grabbed it.

They were seated in Alastair's black SUV. The older man drove as he described the informant.

"She's a great gal. I've known her for years. She's a thirty-two-year veteran operations manager for the Red Hook Port in Brooklyn. Quite a character, makes a delicious stew. Do you like stew?"

"No," Wes said sullenly. "You allege that she's a witch."

"I don't allege anything. She is a witch."

"So is she a Davina or a Willa?" A gentle rain pattered against the windshield. The lights looked unfocused and softer.

"She's Davina, through and through." Alastair turned on his wipers. They streaked across the window, smearing the view so that everything looked as muddled as Wes's mind.

Wes glanced at Alastair, asking sarcastically, "So can I look her in the eye? She won't suck out my soul?"

"Indeed," Alastair replied, but he said nothing else.

The silence thickened until Wes squirmed uncomfortably. "All right, so what did"—Wes checked the information in the folder— "Junie 'Bags' Meadows do to earn this visit from the Witches Protection Program?"

CHAPTER TWO

RED HOOK, BROOKLYN

The cavernous building was covered corner to corner with corrugated shipping containers. They were stacked on top of one another, high enough that some grazed the ceiling. They were brand-new and painted with a logo known to most women throughout the world. Pendragon Cosmetics was a lower-end cosmetic brand found in most drugstores. Heavily advertised on both radio and television, the products promised youth and beauty at a price that made them veritable household items.

A squat woman wearing a polyester skirt and a vest-like apron covered in shamrocks walked down an alley of containers, a clipboard under her arm and a pen designed to look like a tree branch in her gnarled hand. She had unkempt, mousy hair, with a tortoiseshell barrette holding it back from her pallid cheeks. Puffy, purple-colored bags stretched the skin under her eyes. Spider veins created a road map on her flabby face, and most would call her ugly. Junie "Bags" Meadows didn't mind. She had a magic mirror at home, so it didn't matter. Walking confidently toward a milling group, she handed out sheaves of papers to each one of them. Some had questions that she answered patiently, while others stopped to talk office chitchat. The loudspeaker squawked, interrupting conversations.

"Junie. My office, now!"

"Dominic," Junie muttered, exchanging glances with her colleague.

"He sounds pissed," the other woman offered.

Junie shrugged indifferently. "He's a pain in my ass."

Junie walked slowly toward the metal steps leading to the boss's office on the mezzanine. She rushed for no one, man or beast. She rested her hand on the railing and looked up the sixteen steps to the office with a sigh, wondering what the hell he wanted from her. He knew she hated climbing those steps. Looking longingly at a push broom in the corner, she dismissed using magic. *Too many workers here today. Makes them crazy when I do a little something to make my life easier. Upsets the dock-workers, they didn't understand magic—superstitious morons.* She'd been told to keep her powers to herself, anyway. Pendragon was firm about that. While Dominic knew she was a witch, it didn't mean it was public knowledge. Wearily, she climbed the steps, not even her misshapen orthopedic shoes easing her way. "This better be good, Dominic," she muttered as she entered the office. "Whatsamatter, Dominic? The Panama shipments just came in." She slammed the door behind her so hard that the glass windows rattled.

"Why were you going through the Pendragon Cosmetics order?" Dominic demanded. He was forty-four, with a potbelly and dyed black hair with a matching mustache under his very long, cucumber-shaped nose. His gray had come in, so it looked like both his scalp and 'stache had a thin ring of white outlining their shape.

Junie looked at him insolently one hand on her hip. "Because that's my job."

Dominic held up a handful of timecards, waving them around, his face mottled. *A little too choleric before ten in the morning,* Junie observed.

"You called in extra office staff for the export order without asking? That's gotta be canceled."

"Are you kidding me? It's four hundred million units. I can't process that order by myself."

"Well, you better. That's what we pay you for." He threw the cards at her. They fluttered around the office, wafting to the floor like helicopter seeds falling from maple trees. Junie narrowed her eyes at him, her face darkening. "Send 'em home. Did you share this information with anyone?"

"I was in the process of giving it out." She kicked a timecard that landed on her foot. "Why?"

"Go get the manifests back, and I hope for your sake that none of this information gets out." Dominic pounded the desk.

"Why?" Junie repeated, her voice steely.

"Because they don't want it shared with anyone. And it better not have left the building. If it did, there's gonna be some serious consequences."

"You threatening me?" Junie touched the reassuring surface of her pen. It hummed to life, glowing faintly and warming the palm of her hand. She slid it under the chrome clip of the clipboard.

Dominic walked around the desk, bending down to angrily pick up the timecards. He shoved them onto her clipboard, his face close to hers. His fingertips came in contact with her vibrating wand. He brushed together his hands dismissively. "Yeah," he said, his beady eyes holding hers. "I ain't afraid of you or one of your stupid spells, Bags, and neither is Pendragon. You can wind up your magic pen all you want. You got nuthin' against them. You hear me? Nuthin'" His ferret nose quivered with anger as he gave her a final push toward the door.

He stopped, abruptly adding, "Yeah, and by the way, they called earlier and said you better have the galley's victuals and water stocked by Friday."

"I've got a week to get that done!" Junie retorted.

"No, you don't. They want it now, so you got forty-eight hours, you hear me?" He finished with a menacing glare.

"Forty-eight hours?" Junie sputtered, holding up her hand in defeat. "Whoever heard of such a thing? Food's gonna spoil."

"Not your business. Don't make me come and check on you."

Junie nodded, her gaze never leaving his. She walked down the steps, pausing to look up at him watching her intently like an angry vulture. Looking down at her wand, she felt it pulse weakly, knowing her brand of magic was nothing against a giant like Pendragon. Suddenly, Junie was afraid—very afraid. Shivering involuntarily, she went to send her staff home.

CHAPTER THREE

Junie lit a cigarette as soon as she took off her coat. Kicking off her shoes, she put on matted white slippers that made a *whooshing* sound as she paced her tiny apartment. She lived under the tracks, never noticing the train that shook the walls when it raced past her home. It was a four-story, rent-controlled walk-up with hallways that smelled of cabbage and dirty sneakers. There was so much paint on the walls that it made the rooms feel smaller than they were. Luna snaked her black feline body through her mistress's legs, meowing loudly. Junie threw herself on the couch and idly caressed the cat, enjoying the deep purring response. She rested there, letting Luna's calming purrs relax her. Luna smiled up at her, her green eyes warm. Junie felt her tension ease. She rose and walked over to the blotchy mirror that dominated her living room. Despite its faded glitter, it was an elegant accessory, all Rococo in design, with two *putti* angels perched on the top of the frame. She searched the misty depths, staring at her reflection. She touched the swollen pouches under her eyes with a tentative finger.

"Mirror, mirror on the wall." She rolled the words on her tongue.

A deep voice chuckled. "Droll, Bags. Very droll."

"Works in the story." Junie shrugged, her face breaking into a sly smile. She considered her reflection. She needed a change. "I don't like my hair."

The faded brown locks rearranged themselves into a smart blonde chignon. The face in the mirror morphed, the nose delicately flaring as sparkling eyes narrowed. Junie's manicured nails touched her now-porcelain skin. "That's better."

"Agreed," the mirror answered.

"So, can you tell me where this is all going?" she asked the mirror.

"You mean at work, Bags? I only do hair, skin, and nails. You know that."

"Yeah, I know that." Junie shrugged. "That's not going to do me a whole lot of good. Time to make some stew."

Junie winked, then went into her kitchen and pulled out a huge, dented aluminum pot. Pleasant domestic sounds of running water and clattering utensils filled the kitchen. Soon, the whole house smelled of a home-cooked meal. Luna jumped onto the counter, her yowls filling the room. Junie pointed her knife as she answered her pet.

"I know. He was an asshole."

The cat meowed for a long minute. Junie cocked her head. "I called Alastair as soon as I got out of work. You think I waited too long?" The cat growled from deep in its throat. Junie pulled her pen from her apron, fingering the worn wood of her wand. "I know it's weak, but at least it's Davina," she told the cat.

The cat hissed, then leaped off the counter, leaving the room in a huff.

"I ain't afraid, Luna." She paused, taking a deep drag on her cigarette. "I mean, not much."

While the mirror in the parlor reflected back a slender, beautiful woman, in the harsh light of the kitchen window, anybody could see Bags's wrinkled visage. She poured liquid into the big pot, stirring slowly until her craggy face could be seen on the surface of the bubbling stew. Rooting through assorted jars and vials, she added ingredients to the simmering stock, watching images form to replace hers: a young blond man with a close-cropped military cut. She didn't recognize him. Next was a dark-haired girl. It was a witch girl Junie knew. Finally, Alastair's chubby build raced over the eddies and whirlpools that simmered back at her.

Luna meowed loudly. "I know," Junie replied. "I was thinking I needed that, too." She reached high over her head and dumped an entire box of white powder into the pot, watching it circle until it disappeared into the boiling mess. The room turned shades of phosphorus green; her face illuminated by the noxious contents of the pot. A fuzzy image of a head materialized. "Turn around, turn around …" Junie urged. The head rotated, but its features were vague. Junie gasped, blinking twice, when a knock on the door broke the spell.

Another rap. Junie cursed. She wasn't sure, she just wasn't sure of the face. She'd have to re-create the brew to get a better look.

Wes wrinkled his nose at the odors filling the cramped hallway. There was no air to breathe. A short, frumpy woman smoking a cigarette cracked the door enough to peek outside.

"Alastair." Her voice was deep with a strong Brooklyn

accent. "Who's that?" she asked as she opened the door. She poked her head out to scan the corridor. "You followed?"

"Bags." Alastair's voice was friendly. He left his umbrella at the door. "What am I, a rookie? This is my new partner." He walked confidently into the living room, stopping at a large, dense mirror dominating the cramped space. He leaned forward, his white teeth showing with a pleasant smile, stroking his gray goatee. "He's the rookie," he said, gesturing to Wes.

"I am not," Wes said.

"He's greener than a banana just plucked off a banana tree."

"What's that supposed to mean?" Wes asked, slightly off-balance as a black cat twirled itself between his legs. He could feel the vibrations of its purring.

"Faithless jade," Alastair told the cat, whose bright green eyes glared at him. He turned to the older woman. "I've been waiting a long time for this."

"I told you, good things come to those who wait." Junie waved them into a cramped kitchen. There was a table the size of a postage stamp, with an old-fashioned oilcloth attached to it. A pen shaped like a broken twig was thrown carelessly on it. Wes looked closer. *Ha,* he thought with a laugh, thinking it might have been a wand. A black plastic cat clock that hung on the wall ticked, his eyes and tail swinging in synchronized, opposite directions. The movement caught Wes's eyes, and he stood frozen, caught in its hypnotic movements. Alastair snapped his fingers in front of Wes, pulling him out of his trance-like state.

He nodded to the older woman, mouthing, "I told you so."

She approached them both. The overcrowded room made Wes sweat. He backed away, but she moved closer, her eyes half closed. Soon Wes's back made contact with the sticky wallpaper of her kitchen wall. He looked uncomfortably at the water-stained ceiling.

"You can look at me, honey." She gave a wheezy laugh. "I ain't a Willa. He's cute, Alastair." *And familiar,* she thought, knowing his was the first face she had seen in her concoction. Crooked fingers touched his cheek, her yellowed nails scratching his five o'clock shadow. Wes recoiled, pulling his face away. Junie shrugged, sighed, and then walked to the two-burner stove to stir a giant pot with a wooden spoon.

Horrid smells filled the kitchen. Wes looked longingly at the window, knowing there was crisp air outside this nuthouse.

"What's cooking, Bags?" Alastair asked. He glanced in the pot.

"Nothing good, and I'm not talking about my stew." She reached up, her hand grasping air, and flicked her empty palm into the bubbling liquid.

"Ah, a little bit of this," Alastair offered.

"And that." She looked at him pointedly. "I want an upstate cabin."

"Of course."

"One hundred fifty K a year."

"I can't, Junie. Way over budget."

"This is big—bigger and badder than you can imagine."

Alastair looked at her, then replied, "You won't be able to go right away." He thought for a moment. "I'll have to go higher. Only a few more days."

Junie nodded, a silent message passing between them. "You do that." She took out a brown bottle, crusty with dried, dripping fluids running down its filthy sides. "What?" She glanced at Wes's horrified face. "It's good for flavor. You're gonna like it."

Wes gulped, then said, "Alastair said you mentioned something about a face cream when you called earlier." He had read about it in her file.

The older man smiled with approval. Wes looked over at him and said, "I know how to interrogate a witness."

"Indeed." Alastair nodded.

Wes's lips tightened with anger. *Smug bastard,* he thought. He turned all of his attention to Junie.

Junie took a deep drag on her cigarette, then tossed the butt into her pot. "There's a shipment. It's being exported to Singapore, Rio de Janeiro, Southampton, Bremen, and Cape Town."

"Who's moving?" Wes picked up her pen, trying it on his pad. Junie walked over and took the twig from his fingers, her eyes suspicious. She watched him for a tense minute.

"Use your own," she said through her teeth. Wes shrugged, but Alastair wagged a finger.

"Etiquette, Wes. Never touch another person's wand."

"Yeah," Junie added. "You never know where it's been."

Wes wiped his hand down his pants leg, then produced his own pen from his pocket, clicked it loudly, and prepared to take notes. "So," he said after taking a deep breath, "who's moving?"

"Pendragon," Junie told him dismissively.

"The cosmetics company. So?"

"Yeah, well, we've had their contract for over twenty years."

"What's the problem?" Wes asked curtly, looking up at her.

"Four hundred million units of Pendragon Glow face cream? And that's just export. I hear they have another two hundred million being released here in the States as well."

Alastair whistled softly. The cat meowed in agreement. It jumped up on the counter, its tail brushing against Wes's chest. He pushed it away, surprised at its strength.

"What's the big deal if they release a product here?" Wes asked.

"It's never done together," Alastair informed him with a shrug. "Different markets are tested, then sometimes the product is tweaked for the area. Four hundred million units, you said?" Alastair looked concerned.

"Is that a lot?" Wes turned to Junie.

"Biggest I've ever seen. They want the order out pronto. Usually it can take four months to get through channels for export; this was greenlit in two weeks." The cat growled. "Relax, Luna, I'll get to that." Junie was warming to telling her story.

Wes could swear she cracked a smile on her rubbery face. He looked at the animal and then at Junie.

"It got even weirder when I arranged for help in processing the order. They kicked everybody off the dock and made me swear nobody saw the manifest."

Talk about getting weirder. "Who's *they?*" Wes inquired without looking up. He was busy writing.

"My boss, Dominic Cerillo. The thing is, it's gonna take me weeks to complete, but they said I can't have any help. It's almost impossible."

"Did they ask you to use magic?" Alastair asked.

"No, that's the odd part. They're giving the impression they are using legitimate channels." She paused, her protuberant eyes thoughtful. "But that's what it is—an illusion. Something is not right. Something stinks, and it starts with that Pendragon Glow face cream." She paused, remembering something else. "Oh, yeah. They want all the catering loaded by the end of this week. I finished that entire work order today. Very peculiar, if you ask me." Junie opened a cabinet, causing a waterfall of faded plastic containers to cascade onto her head. Wes automatically bent to help pick them up. Junie smiled, purring, "Nice boy."

"Why?"

"Why, what?" Junie asked distractedly.

"Why is that peculiar?" Wes asked.

"It means they want those cargo ships ready to leave on their schedule. They're leaving nothing to chance," Alastair said thoughtfully. "Something does smell funny."

Wes wrinkled his nose, thinking something indeed smelled,

and he was pretty sure it started with whatever she was cooking in that battered pot.

"What are you preparing there?" Wes pointed to the bubbling concoction that was now bathing the room with oily steam.

Junie raised the spoon to her pursed mouth and sampled the green liquid, making great slurping sounds as she tried it. "Protection. I'm brewing protection. Want some?" She held out a spoon dripping with a boiling, slimy mess. She poured some into the canister, handing it to Alastair. "For later," she said with a wink. She smiled, revealing a mouthful of tobacco-stained teeth.

Wes recoiled, but Alastair calmly said, "That's what we're here for." He politely took the package from her.

Junie nodded, her gaze moving to the window. She wiped her hands down her filthy apron. She thought briefly about sharing what she saw in her brew, but she wasn't sure—she just wasn't sure. "I always trusted you, Alastair, but I think we have to move fast." She scuttled back to the stove and made an identical canister for Wes.

"I couldn't." Wes backed away, shaking his head.

"You can, and you will," Alastair said, plucking the container from Junie's hand and handing it to Wes. "Very gracious, Junie. It will do him good." He smiled benignly at the old crone. "I will have to find a good place where I can hide you for a few days. You know, until I setup something more permanent. Someone will be by to collect you in"—he looked at his watch— "in about thirty-six hours."

"That long?" Junie asked, her face worried.

Alastair shrugged. "Paperwork. Take the minimum; travel light."

Junie nodded, staring out the window worriedly. Wes

wondered why she was so nervous. If this was all believable, wasn't she a witch too? Wouldn't her powers protect her?

Alastair spoke as though he could read Wes's thought. "Every witch has different powers. The good ones are predictable. They dabble with helpful spells, medicine—you know, things to enrich one's life."

"That's the thing," Junie said, turning to look at Wes. "I would never hurt a fly—not a fly! You can't trust a Willa. They dance to their own drum. They don't care about anything!"

"Do you have any contacts at Pendragon?" Wes asked.

Bags shook her head. "I smell a Willa spell brewing. Check out the girl."

"What girl?" Wes asked, noticing their exchange.

The older woman looked at Alastair, who shrugged.

"You know, the one in all the tabloids."

"What's her name?" Wes looked up and noticed Alastair's troubled gaze.

Junie didn't answer. A raven cawed, and the old crone hissed. Hunching over, she peered outside, the full moon painting her face with an evil yellow glow. She squinted; her wrinkled lips twitched, turning her face into a macabre mask. Wes shuddered, wondering, *If she is a good witch, what does a bad one look like?*

"Let's go," Alastair said tersely. "I'll get this moving as fast as I can, Bags."

Wes spun, catching the reflection of a beautiful girl in the mirror in the parlor. He swiveled, looking for another person, only to see Junie "Bags" Meadows's gaunt face gazing into the mirror intently, her wand clutched in her shaking grasp.

"Who's the girl?" Wes asked as soon as they got into the car.

Alastair turned the ignition without answering.

"I asked, who's the girl?" Wes demanded, forcing Alastair to look at him.

"Morgan. Morgan Pendragon."

The rest of the ride was eerily silent.

By the time Alastair dropped him off at home, it was past eleven. Wes opened the fridge, deciding it was too late to eat anything. He left the plastic container on his Formica counter, the greenish glow illuminating his darkened kitchen. He picked it up, feeling the lingering warmth. It hummed and throbbed, the liquid inexplicably churning. He looked longingly at the trash, but for some reason he couldn't explain, he decided not to chuck it.

CHAPTER FOUR

The sun loved the Avenue of the Americas. Halal vendors lined the street. The smell of roasting meat clashed with the fumes of hundreds of cars. A cart filled with fruits and nuts was parked itself by the entrance of the eighty-story skyscraper. There was never any space in front of the building. It was always packed with mail trucks, car services, and the ubiquitous food wagons. Morgan Pendragon directed the driver to stop so she could jump out before the green awning of her family's building. The gunmetal Escalade inched closer, but traffic was at a standstill. The driver turned around, a look of apology on his face.

"Never mind. It's just a few feet, Omar. I'll get out here."

She heard the driver calling for her to wait as she opened the door, descending to the pavement. She was little, just over five feet tall, and wondered why she didn't insist they buy a smaller, more fuel-efficient car for the company. Her aunt loved this big monster; Morgan guessed it made her feel powerful. She tapped the door, letting him know she was outside already.

Omar lowered the window. Morgan jumped onto the curb, stretching so she could see him.

"Don't wait for me. I'll call if I need a ride home." She heard him yelling something to her, but his words were lost in the daytime racket of city life. Hugging her hobo bag close to her body, Morgan passed the engraved stone slab identifying Pendragon Global Headquarters and entered the building through the revolving doors. Gleaming marble floors that reflected the first of many banks of elevators greeted her. The lobby was five stories high with soaring ceilings framed by steel beams. A large marble console ten feet long was in the center, staffed with a row of uniformed receptionists to greet newcomers. Huge television screens hung suspended from the tall ceilings, all of them playing commercials for the new face cream her aunt was launching. Morgan shuddered as she watched the model slather white paste onto her creamy complexion. The girl glowed with vitality. The next scene showed how the cream enhanced lives, rapidly flashing women in power suits, commanding naval ships, getting awards. Morgan muttered the tagline: "Pendragon: For the glow of success." *Unholy crap*, she thought.

Two security guards nodded as she hurried past the line waiting to be given passes to enter the building. She weaved through the crowds, sprinting along three corridors, and arrived at a final elevator that went exclusively to the eighty-fifth-floor penthouse.

The doors opened with a soft hiss to purple carpet and black marble walls. The Pendragon logo was both in the center of the floor and on the wall, a metal plaque of an impressionistic cauldron, a wisp of steam rising above it.

She smiled at the receptionist, walking briskly to the inner office. Jasmine, her aunt's personal assistant, rose from her sleek desk. Morgan admired Jasmine's beautiful skin, smooth as caramel. Her black hair was in a neat ponytail at the base of her slender neck.

"Great skirt." Morgan smiled, knowing Bernadette insisted her staff dress in designer clothes. It drove her aunt nuts that she chose vintage thrift-store finds.

She watched the secretary's brown eyes travel up her Doc Martens to her ripped black pants and oversized, washed-out, midnight Black Sabbath shirt. Morgan loved how Ozzy's eyes followed everyone. Her dark hair was disheveled; she knew she needed to brush the wild locks back into place.

Jasmine looked at the double door and turned to the younger girl. "I keep an extra pair of shoes here. Do you want to borrow them?" she asked kindly.

Morgan lowered her heavy bag onto the desk with a thud. "You don't like my boots?"

"A little *Mad Max* for me."

"Yeah, Bea's going to hate them."

Jasmine smiled nervously. "I'll buzz her. She's on the phone."

"No need." Morgan hefted her purse onto her shoulder and walked with deliberation into her aunt's inner sanctum.

Floor-to-ceiling windows greeted her, sunlight drenching the steel-colored carpet. There was a polished quartz table that could seat thirty people to the left and a black leather couch shaped in a half circle to the right. Crystals from an oversize chandelier hung overhead, looking like suspended icicles. Morgan remembered the light fixture had cost almost a million dollars. A huge branch from a willow tree was tacked to the wall, green buds inexplicably sprouting on the disconnected limb. On opposite walls, there was original artwork—giant canvases with black slashes that gave the impression of swirling movement.

Her aunt's desk was at center stage, made from some sort of

colorless, polished stone. Morgan knew it never showed her aunt's fingerprints. Witches didn't have them. Three smooth rocks of various sizes were piled on the corner of the desk. They were different shades of red, from rust to a pale pink. Morgan's eyes were always drawn to them.

Bernadette Pendragon ignored the intrusion. Her gaze was focused on a sheaf of papers on the desk while she listened to someone talking on the phone. Morgan could hear that the speaker was distressed by the urgency and the rapid conversation she heard through the receiver. Bernadette's beautiful face was mildly bored. She had straight black hair, shaped like a cap, cut close to her skull. High cheekbones, slashes for brows, and a tight line painted with her signature red lipstick made her as unapproachable as her cold smile did. She was reed thin, bordering on emaciated, Morgan always thought. Everything about her screamed power, from her economy of movement to her equally sparse way of speaking. She glanced up, her cold gray eyes flicking over Morgan's outfit, then she turned her attention to the folder Scarlett, her other assistant, held out for approval.

"Juliet," Bernadette said briskly into the phone. "I told you not to worry. You do your job, and I'll handle the rest." There was a heavy pause on the other end, then a spate of words. Clearly, Juliet was not happy. Bernadette wrote something on a pad and moved aside for Scarlett to read it. She underscored the words. Scarlett nodded, her toady smile reassuring her boss. "Juliet," Bernadette said sharply. "Start behaving like the leader you were born to be!" There was a pause. "I understand." Bernadette examined her pen. "I will take care of that."

"Who's that?" Morgan asked, her voice low.

Bernadette hung up, her faraway gaze directed to the floor to ceiling windows. "She's out of control," she said, more to herself than anyone else in the room. Turning to Scarlett, she continued, "Contact Reeva in Washington and tell her to keep an eye on ..." Bernadette paused, staring at her niece, her face unreadable.

"Yes, of course. I know what to do, Bernadette," Scarlett responded.

Lush and curvy, Scarlett was squeezed into a tight black dress. Her blonde hair framed her round, artfully made-up face. Scarlett sneered at Morgan. Morgan felt her skin redden—*Oh, the curse of fair skin,* she thought. Scarlett hated her, and for the life of her, Morgan couldn't figure out why.

Morgan cleared her throat. "Morning, Aunt Bea." Pointedly ignored, Morgan tried again. "Morning, Aunt Bernadette."

Bernadette placed her pen down carefully, resting her spider hands on the face of the desk. "Get a latte for my niece," she said, dismissing the assistant. Scarlett's eyes narrowed to slits that appeared to steam, but this was apparently unnoticed by the mogul. Morgan swallowed convulsively.

"Why are you here? Don't you have"—Bernadette consulted a computer screen— "a political science class now?" She looked at the leather chair, then at her niece, who took the invitation to slide into it. "Don't slouch, Morgan."

Morgan straightened. "The professor got sick."

Scarlett returned with a clear glass of coffee, a precise amount of foam floating on the top.

"Cast a spell?" Scarlett asked snidely.

"Thanks." Morgan took the steaming cup, sipping it cautiously. "You know I don't like to use witchcraft."

"Pity." Scarlett enjoyed a certain amount of freedom being Bernadette's assistant. She was a few years older than Morgan, and her family had known the Pendragons for eons. She started as an intern and had gotten the job when Bernadette's former assistant had broken her hip in a terrible fall.

"She'll grow into it." Bernadette's eyes glowed, but her smile was brittle. "I didn't waste my time teaching you to use our craft for cleaning your room or playing tricks with your little friends." She eyed her niece's chipped purple nails with disgust. "The least you could do is change your polish. I mean it—do it now, Morgan."

Morgan looked out the window, sighing with resignation when her aunt added, "If you don't, I will, and I promise you won't like the color."

Morgan reached into her bag, pulling out a bent-looking twig. She regarded it fondly. It was her mother's. Bernadette's lips turned down when she spotted it. Morgan whispered a few words, twirling it in the air, and a fresh coat of purple polish covered her nails. Her aunt nodded with approval.

Bernadette stood, languidly walking around the desk. She perched herself on the corner, swinging a long, black-clad leg. Picking up the smallest of the rocks, she held it in her hand, then rubbed the pink surface with her thumb. Her eyes sharpened as she stared at her niece. The room took on a warm-and-fuzzy glow. "Anyway, you should be spending your time practicing how to fly."

"I don't want to fly, thank you very much," Morgan replied, a mutinous pout on her lips. Much as she wanted to be rebellious, she felt forced to relax, the lambent light making her drowsy.

"Every witch flies," Scarlett told her condescendingly.

Morgan shrugged. "I don't like talking about …"

Bernadette pinned her niece with an amused stare. "What?"

"You know."

"No, I don't know." Bernadette let the pink rock roll onto the desk. She picked up the next largest. The room buzzed with electricity, pushing Morgan from her slight stupor.

"Yes, you do, Bea," Morgan said impatiently. "I don't like to talk about … spells. Or witching. I don't want to fly, and I don't like to cast spells. Well, not many."

Bernadette's thin lips shaped into a slight smile. "What we are is not just for fun, Morgan. You use magic when it suits your needs. Don't shake your head. I know you do." She cut off Morgan's protest, her hand gripping the rock.

Morgan knew her aunt was correct. Magic was entertainment, nothing more. She had a wand, of course; it was her mother's. She used it only with her friend, Gabby, when they *really, really* needed to.

Magic was a responsibility that she didn't want. Morgan looked warily at the three rocks that had moved to the center of Bernadette's desk.

Bernadette smile. "Come now, you know they are decoration. They don't have any magic." She reached into her bottom drawer and took out an ancient book. "This does. One day, this will be yours."

It was old, at least five hundred years, with a rusted metal clasp, the vellum pages rippled with age. The cover had faded lettering in a language Morgan could only guess at. She swore she could smell the decayed tome from where she sat. Morgan shook her head. "I don't want it."

"Practicing magic is your birthright. You will have to accept that one day. You can't pick and choose what you like about it. I have collected spells for over thirty years." She rested her hand on the book. "This is the culmination of them."

Morgan shrugged indifferently. "Maybe I'll give the whole thing up."

"Don't talk blasphemy. Once you are born with the gift, it is yours forever. Be that as it may, as long as you are here, I'll have Jasmine bring in the papers." Bernadette pressed the buzzer.

"What papers?" Morgan rose.

"The ones you were supposed to sign last week." Bernadette

picked up the stone again, her hand squeezing it gently. Morgan's gaze moved to her aunt's fist and the light-colored rock.

Morgan looked at Scarlett, then back at her aunt. "Can't we talk about this in private?"

Bernadette motioned for Scarlett to leave. Scarlett huffed off, clearly annoyed at the dismissal.

"I don't understand why you are insisting I sign them."

"As both CEO of this company and your parental guardian, it is my duty to ensure that you are protected."

"I am turning twenty-one. I don't need to be protected." Morgan got up to pace the room but felt defeated already. "It's my company, too," she complained.

"Sit down, Morgan," Bernadette said softly. She patted the seat of the chair. "I said, *sit down.*" There was a note of steel in her voice that could not be ignored.

"You're asking me to sign away the company."

"That's not true. Just your voting rights. You are too young to vote."

"I am the same age as you and my mother were when you created this company," Morgan shot back.

"You are a child, Morgan," Bernadette said dismissively.

"And you're controlling."

"Yes." Bernadette put down the stone in its proper place with a click, then went back to her chair. "It gets the job done. If I were a man, everybody would marvel at my aggression. I'd be called a *go-getter*, ambitious. People would respect me. However, I am a woman, so I am controlling and bossy and dictatorial. I have to be; otherwise Pendragon would be a two-bit makeup company. It's the only way to be taken seriously. I can see by your face that you understand that."

"We should be doing something for humanity," Morgan

said hotly. "We are privileged and have a responsibility to help people, spread our good fortune to further society."

Bernadette laughed at her. "You want to stay privileged, my little princess, don't you?"

"We have more than enough," Morgan declared, her brows drawn.

"I should cut you off and see how benevolent you feel then," Bernadette said condescendingly. "Make you see the truth. Without money, I'm talking about real money, we are nothing. When your mother was killed, we were doing two million in sales. Today our market cap is seventy-five *billion*. Your mother never had vision."

"And you do," said Morgan. She stood by the window, looking out on the tiny cars moving below. It was quiet up here, high in the clouds. On the other side of the river was Jersey and its vast complex of Pendragon warehouses.

"Of course," Bernadette responded confidently.

"That wasn't a question."

"It doesn't matter. You like having your loft in SoHo, the private driver, your expensive trailer-trash clothes. Sign the documents, and you can continue as you always have."

"It's all just stuff."

"So you say," Bernadette said smugly.

"Why is it so important that I sign?" Morgan's dark eyes filled with tears.

"I want to see women all over the world using Pendragon Glow. We are having a global release that can't be interrupted with new people sticking their inexperienced noses in my business."

"Oh, that snake oil again. Please, Bernadette, take it off the market. You know as well as I do it just barely got through the FDA."

"A mere formality. I know what I'm doing, Morgan. The cream will revolutionize the beauty industry."

"Like the Segway revolutionized walking. It's a face cream! Not the cure for cancer. I just don't like anything about it. I don't like the way it smells, the way it feels. It's a bad product, Bea."

"You see? You see why you have to sign now? You don't understand its importance. It's ultra-nourishing, deeply hydrating. Its unique formula will change the way women see themselves."

"It's poison, and you know it, Bea."

"Why would you even say that? You never complained about our products before."

"Because this cream is different. Because you're different since you started developing it." Morgan turned thoughtful. "You've been so secretive about it. You are up to something. I just don't know what."

Bernadette stood, her six-foot frame towering over her petite niece. She placed her thin hand on Morgan's shoulder, her mouth close to her ear. "You are too young to be involved. We are the fastest-growing company in the world. Women everywhere are begging for more. We have to empower our consumers. Give them control over their lives. This new line has a little bit of … you and me in it."

"What are you talking about?"

"DNA. We are raising the bar in cosmetics! We are changing the world."

"That's revolting." Morgan turned. "The only one who will have control is you. It's sick, sick!" Morgan bolted to get her bag, but her aunt's strident voice stopped her. She was holding her stone again. Morgan froze as if an invisible rope connected them.

"We have been oppressed for centuries. We've had to hide our true abilities from the world."

"Davinas don't have to hide."

Bernadette's lips made a moue of disapproval. "It's time for us to function the way we were designed."

"You're talking like a Willa." Morgan's voice was a hushed whisper.

"Do you think all this"—Bernadette's arms opened wide, the rock in her fisted hand, to indicate the opulent office— "came from behaving like a Davina?"

"You and my mother are Davina. We are Davinas, as was Grandmama and her mother before that."

"You are so naïve." Bernadette smiled sadly. "This grows tiresome." She picked up a black-and-white photo of a young woman who looked like a younger version of herself. "Poor, poor Catarina. She was so cautious, so … pious."

"You're wicked," Morgan accused her.

"If the shoe fits."

"Wrong fairy tale. I'm leaving."

"Sign the papers, Morgan, or I'll make your life miserable." Bernadette hit the intercom. "Jasmine, have my niece sign the papers I gave you earlier."

The door opened, and Scarlett escorted two other women into the room. Both were extremely tall, dwarfing Scarlett. One was Asian; the other had the dark hair and olive skin of the Mediterranean. Both were dressed in black leather. They took up spots on either side of the room like silent sentinels. Morgan knew them and disliked them equally. Wu came from China and dealt with the factories in Asia. She was her aunt's liaison with the production centers. Proud and hawkish, she refused to exchange pleasantries, no matter how anyone tried. She had a superior air that kept people at a distance, including Morgan. Vincenza had started as an exchange student from Italy and somehow never left. She had predatory eyes and a sneaky countenance. She worked as an errand girl for her aunt, and many times Morgan and Vincenza had been thrown together while waiting for Bernadette. Once, her aunt had sent the two of them to the Bronx Zoo, and Vincenza had creeped her out with her fascination in the reptile house. Somehow, she'd found a way inside to lie down with a python, and Morgan had to call her aunt to order her out before the zookeeper found her. Morgan nodded coldly to both of them.

"There's been a problem with the shipment," Scarlett told Bernadette as she approached the desk.

"Not now, Scarlett." She looked at Morgan, her gaze warning her. "Sign the papers today." Her voice was quiet.

"Or what?" Morgan asked defiantly.

"You don't want to know."

Jasmine sat at her desk, a pile of papers three inches thick in front of her.

"Do you want to sit here?" Jasmine said, apologetically holding out a pen.

Morgan moved to leave. Jasmine smiled sadly. "I have to have those papers signed. I'm sorry, Morgan."

Morgan pursed her lips. If her aunt insisted she embrace her inner witch, then the old bat was going to have to deal with the consequences. Reaching into her hobo bag, she moved the contents around. "I only use my own pen."

"Excuse me," Jasmine said playfully. "Is it special?"

"It was my mom's." Morgan continued searching the voluminous bag. Her short fingers found the cylindrical shape of her willow wand, and she closed her eyes with regret. Saying a silent apology to Jasmine, she whispered, "You never saw me leave.

I'm getting off the hook. Place these stupid papers in a place no one will ever look."

The air between them crackled and buzzed

Jasmine's eyes glazed as she took the pile of papers, putting them in a cabinet in the corner of her office. Morgan said a breezy goodbye as the elevator doors closed. Jasmine blinked rapidly, looked around distractedly, and then sat down to type a memo.

CHAPTER FIVE

S unlight bleached the pavement an ivory white. Wes sat in Alastair's SUV. There were two half-filled coffee cups and a half-dozen doughnuts between them. The morning rush swirled around the car. New York City in the early morning had a special, infectious energy. People jogged in shorts and tank tops; women wore skirts, their feet in comfortable sneakers, their high heels hanging from the openings of their purses. Men in business suits, swinging briefcases, rushed past the car, sometimes holding the hands of the small children they escorted to school before work.

The two agents watched as the March winds stirred the brisk air, making people walk with a snap in their step.

Wes felt something weighty bounce in his lap and fall to the floor of the car. He turned to Alastair. "What was that?"

"Pick it up."

Squeezing his large shoulders between the dash and the floor, he combed the floor mat until his hands closed on a cold metal object. Picking it up, he held a badge pinned to a leather patch held by a long chain.

"You've gotta be kidding me," Wes said.

His thumb caressed the embossed shield, which displayed two crossed broomsticks and the name *Witches Protection Program*. His eyes rested on the bottom of the shield where the motto announced "Defenders of the Craft" in bold letters.

He turned to Alastair. "Defenders of the Craft?"

Alastair replied, "Indeed."

Wes dropped the badge negligently into his jacket pocket, forgetting about it immediately.

Alastair handed Wes a long, thin box. "Here, your business cards. I had them made for you last night."

Wes shook his head, waving them away. "I won't be needing them. I don't plan on staying long. One and done, and then I'll be heading back to my old unit."

"Of course," Alastair agreed. "Still, you never know. Take a few for the time being."

Wes didn't like Alastair's smug smile. Everything about the older man, who'd picked him up at seven that morning, rubbed him the wrong way. Still, he took out four cards, stuffing them in the inside pocket of his jacket.

"Personally, I'm a jelly man all the way." Alastair popped a doughnut into his mouth, his eyes on the crowd. The little guy irritated him something fierce. Wes grunted a response. He didn't want to make small talk with Alastair, the lucky leprechaun. He didn't want doughnuts—or coffee, for that matter. He wanted to get the job done, go back to his father's department, and never think about a witch again. Not even on Halloween. He pulled out his phone from his pocket, accessed Safari, then silently typed in *Morgan Pendragon*.

"It's like she barely exists," Wes said dispiritedly as he combed popular sites looking for images of the girl.

"Keep looking; she's there," Alastair told him, wiping his

fingertips on a napkin. "She never liked having her picture taken."

"Yeah, she's always hiding behind a big purse or something."

"If you check out anything in the club scene, you'll find her. Stop searching for her. Look for artists, musicians, reality show creatures. She's always in the crowd. Look." He leaned over, pointing his short finger at the screen. Jelly smeared on the surface. "There she is."

Wes gave him a dirty look, rubbing ineffectually at the stain. "Oh, come on, I would never have found her." He clicked on the photo, enlarging the grainy image with his fingers. It was a group of goth-looking freaks outside Faves, a trendy nightclub downtown. He peered closely at a short girl with dark hair, held under the arm of a tall singer from the band Ratfinger. The guy had lumps on his forehead. Wes brought the phone closer to his face.

"Body modification," Alastair told him, his eyes now searching the crowds on the city sidewalks outside the Pendragon building. "They have shapes surgically put under their skin to make themselves look—"

"She's into that?" Wes interrupted as he tried to enlarge her white face.

"Kids," Alastair said with an indifferent shrug. "There she is." He gestured to a pixie of a girl on the sidewalk, dressed all in black, carrying the oversized purse Wes now recognized. "Wait here."

Alastair hopped out of the car. Wes fished his new badge from his pocket, slapped it on the dash, and quickly followed him.

"Miss—Miss Pendragon," Alastair called out to her.

Morgan heard her name being called and spotted an old man and a young, blond hunk following her. She noticed they didn't have cameras, so they weren't paps; maybe they worked for her aunt. Morgan picked up her pace, trying to lose them.

Wes dodged the crowds, outdistancing Alastair in his rush to get to the girl. He stopped short when he realized that not only did the older man have the girl, but he had somehow passed him without notice. Wes looked around wildly. Alastair's calm voice reached him.

"I told you to stay in the car." He had Morgan Pendragon's arm in a grasp that looked casual, but Wes knew from the expression on her face, it was not. "Miss Pendragon, we'd like to have a word with you."

They had to be cops. Morgan eyed the little gray-haired guy with the goatee and the blond Neanderthal following him with the dawning realization they were feds. "Piss off."

"Miss Pendragon, we would like to ask you a few questions."

"Do you have a warrant?" Morgan demanded.

Alastair turned sideways, his trench coat flaring in the breeze. Morgan spied the butt of an antique Vaporizer, and her breath caught in her throat.

"Who are you guys?" she whispered.

"We're friends, Morgan," Alastair told her, his dark eyes boring into hers. "We want to have a chat."

Wes reached into his pocket and was shocked when the girl flinched in fear. "Please don't be alarmed." He gave Alastair's hold on her a dirty look. "I'm only giving you my business card."

Alastair's eyebrow rose with his smirk. Wes glared at him hotly.

Morgan took the card, her body tense. Crumpling it, she threw it into her voluminous bag while she snatched her other hand back from the older man. Morgan swallowed nervously, searching her purse with her fingers. She felt the slender base of her mother's wand and gripped it, muttering, "Come, wind. Stir some dust; mask their eyes. Escape, I must."

"No!" Alastair cried as a swirling mass of grit and dirt surrounded both men, blinding them. Morgan pulled free and was gone in an instant.

Wes rubbed his tearing eyes. "You lost her! What did she do?"

Alastair coughed, wiping his irritated face. He scanned the street, knowing she was gone. He glanced up to see his SUV being hooked onto a city tow truck.

"What the—! I told you to stay with the truck, Wes." He started racing to his vehicle but stopped as it was pulled hastily away and down the street.

"Don't yell at me! I'm not the one who let her go," Wes barked back. He was getting tired of Alastair's air of superiority. Wes leaned over, gasping from both the windstorm and his sprint. "Anyway, I put that stupid badge in the window."

"Yeah. Right. The cops don't recognize us. We fly under the radar."

"What's that supposed to mean?"

"Just what I said. We fly under the radar. Call Bathsheba and tell her to get the car out of impound." Alastair hailed a cab. Wes stopped him.

"Why don't we go in and look around?" Wes gestured at the tall building.

Alastair thought for a moment and then told the cabbie he didn't need him. "You won't get past security. Bernadette is in the penthouse; you'll never get up there."

"Watch me," Wes told him, as if on a dare. "Wait here. I'll be back soon." He walked over to the back of a parcel truck, eyeing a stack of boxes left negligently on the curb. Alastair pointed to the driver, now waiting impatiently by a food truck. Alastair strolled toward the line, placing his bulky body in the driver's line of sight. Wes nodded, grabbing the pile of boxes. "This ought to be interesting." He smiled, feeling proactive. He'd show the old guy he wasn't such a loser.

CHAPTER SIX

W es walked confidently into the entry, the parcels blocking most of his face. He had used a black felt-tip-pen to write Bernadette Pendragon's name as the recipient before walking up to the receptionist.

"Hi," he told the guard. "These have to be signed for."

The guard picked up a pen. Wes moved away. "Not by you. The receiver, um," he said slowly, looking down as if he were reading it for the first time, "Bernadette Pendragon."

The guard looked at the names on the boxes, shrugged, typed something, then handed Wes a sticker with a pass on it. "That's for the thirty-fourth floor, the mailroom."

Wes shook his head. "It says receiver only, says here she's in the penthouse, right? My job, pal, is to get it to them."

The guard picked up a phone, spoke for a second, then hung up. "Penthouse. Last elevator bank."

Wes nodded, then headed for the final elevator. He felt himself filling with confidence during the trip up the eighty floors.

The doors *whooshed* open.

He looked out into the quiet, plush office. A beautiful girl with *café au lait* skin was walking into the reception area as he exited the lift.

"May I help you?" she asked politely.

"Packages for …" Wes pretended to consult the top box, "Bernadette Pendragon."

"Oh, I'll take that." She smiled warmly.

"Wow, big place. A lot of guards just for make-up. They gave me a hard time coming up here." Wes grinned back.

Jasmine shrugged. "Security. You're in rarefied air up here. They don't let just anybody in."

"Guess I'm special." He swept his eyes appreciatively down her body. The girl blushed prettily.

"You might be right," she flirted back.

"Downstairs looks busy. Got anything special going on?"

Jasmine glanced at him sideways, her lashes sweeping her golden cheeks. "Yes, as a matter of fact. They are planning a huge release of face cream … worldwide."

"Face cream? What's the big deal?" Wes asked innocently. He looked at the pretty assistant, his smile widening. "There are thousands of them on the market. They're all the same, if you ask me."

"Oh no." Jasmine's dark eyes sparkled. "This one is unique."

"I don't think you need anything like that. You have pretty skin." He put the boxes on a chest-high reception desk, then leaned closer to Jasmine, a lazy grin on his face.

Jasmine flushed again. "Thanks, you're sweet to say so. No, really, it's been tested." She moved closer so their faces were almost touching, as if to share a secret. She whispered, "It can—"

"Jasmine!" Scarlett's strident voice called, wiping the smile from the pretty girl's face. "What do you think you're doing? All packages are supposed to come in through receiving."

Wes heard the click of sharp heels. He put his hand on his hip and turned to the rude speaker.

She was beautiful and curvy, with blonde hair and pouty red lips. She slowed, her strut becoming languid, but her gaze hardened on Jasmine. "I'll take over. You should know better."

Jasmine's face paled, and her lips thinned. "I need to take the boxes—"

Scarlett's eyes blazed. "I told you to go back to your desk. Don't make me say it again."

Jasmine blanched. Wes recognized primal fear in her face. The air vibrated with it. She hastily began to retreat back to where she'd come from. She glanced around to smile at Wes one more time.

"I said, go!" Scarlett ordered. Jasmine flinched, then scurried off, not looking at him again, the boxes neglected on the desk.

The atmosphere thickened in the entry. Scarlett turned to face him. Her voice changed. Wes could swear she purred. "What do you have there?" She gave a cursory glance at the boxes. Her black skirt hugging her long legs. Wes stood back, admiring the view.

"Like what you see?" she asked. She stood as if posing, then moved toward him. "You know; you're not allowed to come up here."

"Just doing my job, ma'am."

"Ma'am. You make me feel so old," she teased him, wetting her lips. "You could get in a lot of trouble."

"I wouldn't want to cause any problems, especially when you have a big event going on. Are you giving out any samples?" he asked, coming closer.

Scarlett placed a warm hand on his shoulder. Her mouth, came so close to his ear that her breath tickled him. "It's a secret," she whispered.

Wes put his hand on the curve of her hip. "I like secrets," he said back, his voice soft.

"I bet you do," Scarlett responded, her lips grazing his.

Wes knew she was an armful of lushness, but as much as he tried to move toward her, something repelled him. Scarlett looked up at him, sensing his withdrawal, her hand splayed on his chest. They stood toe to toe, their breath intermingling. Wes could feel her sharp intake of breath as though she'd seen something deep in his eyes. She pushed him away. "You ask too many questions, errand boy. I think you should go."

"What about the packages?"

"We don't need you anymore. Security!" she called into the hidden phone she held in her hand. "Come and escort this man out."

She walked away, her gaze lingering on him as two burly guards appeared, taking his arms and directing him none too gently toward the elevator.

"So," Alastair said, offering him a bag of hot chestnuts.

Wes took one, popping it in his mouth. "Security is tight, nothing new in post 9/11 New York."

Alastair nodded.

"It's a strange place." Wes shrugged.

"Indeed. What do you mean?"

"The employee I met was scared. Really scared," said Wes thoughtfully.

CHAPTER SEVEN

Morgan looked behind her back, satisfied they hadn't followed her. She stepped into a recessed door, typed out a text for Gabby, and then headed to her friend's place. It was on Ninth Avenue, a seedy tenement right in the middle of Hell's Kitchen. Gabby lived in the ten-story residence with a creepy, temperamental box as an excuse for an elevator. Many times, they'd sat on the floor of the lift, waiting to be rescued. Morgan had recently asked why the neighborhood was called Hell's Kitchen.

"In the 1800s, it was a rough place to live," Gabby informed her.

"It still is. I don't know how your parents let you stay here."

"They don't have much to say about it. Rent is cheap enough."

The old brown building was squashed between a newer high-rise and a crumbling office building. The apartment reeked of Chinese food being cooked on the first floor.

"You didn't answer my question yesterday about Hell's

Kitchen," Morgan said, kicking off her boots and throwing her bag on the sad Naugahyde sofa.

"Well, they used to say, 'What's hotter than hell?'"

"Hell's Kitchen," Morgan said in unison with Gabby. "Kinda creepy, you living here."

"It works with my image. Chic witch with a practice in Hell's Kitchen." Gabby bowed, her face beaming.

"Yeah, well, first of all, you're not a witch." Morgan held up her hand, ticking off her points.

"Yet. I'm learning," Gabby retorted.

"Second of all, it hasn't been proven that you can even learn to be a witch. My aunt says you have to be born a witch."

"A mere formality. We will prove the skeptics wrong. Some of my spells have worked." Her eyes sparkled, warming Morgan's heart. She loved Gabby. When she had been friendless and alone and no one had wanted to associate with her, Gabby had cheerfully embraced her. "Never mind all that, what happened? Your text was crazy. Who were the guys that stopped you?"

Morgan shivered, thinking about the gun. She had only seen one in a book in their library at Bea's home.

"I don't know, and guess what? I don't want to know. This is all getting scary. First, Bea wants me to sign over my voting rights."

"What is she, Stalin?" Gabby exclaimed as she went into the kitchen to grab bottled water and a bag of chips. "Why is she doing that?"

"Next month is my birthday, right?" Morgan dug into her bag, fishing out the crumpled business card.

"Right, and we're going to Cabo to celebrate!" Gabby fell onto the couch, bringing up a swirl of dust. They both coughed and waved their hands. "What's that?" she said pointing to the business card.

"The guy, the young one who followed me, gave me this." She held out the creased business card.

Gabby smoothed it out. "Wesley Rockville. Was he cute?"

Morgan shrugged. "I suppose, if you like big, blond men with tons of muscles and bright blue eyes," she said dismissively.

"And you ran away from this guy?" Gabby asked, throwing the card into an ashtray.

Morgan leaned over, took out a match, and lit the card. Her eyes were transfixed as the fire curled the paper, turning it to ash. The flame flared upward, sparks flying. Both girls exhaled with surprise.

"Is that magic?" Gabby asked, her eyes wide.

"I—I don't know," Morgan said with uncertainty. Staring at the ashes of the card, the only thing that came to her was a sense of lost opportunity; she had no idea where that thought came from. Morgan blew at the remaining embers, watching them pulse and then go dark. A spray of ash fell on the carpet. She rubbed her fingertip over the embers, making sure they were out. Strangely, the heat traveled through her skin, up her arm, and lodged in the center of her chest. Morgan knew without a doubt it belonged there. She sat back with a look of wonder. "This place is a dive," Morgan gasped, trying unsuccessfully to hide the confusion she was feeling.

"A dump," Gabby added. "Back to the Wicked Witch of the East. Why is she trying to make you sign away your voting rights? You haven't voted for anything yet. You can't until you turn twenty-one. What's she up to, that old enchantress?" Gabby twirled her bright-red hair on her very slender hand. She had milk-white skin, fierce eyes, a turned-up nose, and a dash of cinnamon-colored freckles. She was tall and thin, with a hoop through her delicate eyebrow and a diamond stud implanted in the deep dimple on her right cheek. She'd wanted to be a witch since she was a little girl. Morgan was amused by that. They'd met during freshman year at NYU, and Morgan had tutored her in both math and spells. Gabby couldn't do either. Morgan enjoyed tricking her into believing she had developed powers.

Morgan rested her feet on the giant industrial spool that served as a coffee table. They had found it in the trash by a construction site and had rolled it home. Morgan had used magic to get it up the stairs after it had toppled down twice, waking the super. "I made arrangements so they'll never find those papers."

"You used magic? With your aunt? Did it feel good?" Gabby pulled out a bag of red licorice that was wedged in the cushions. "Yum." She ripped off some, handing it to Morgan.

"No, her assistant." Morgan chewed thoughtfully.

"Who, Scarlett or Frick and Frack?" Gabby asked, referring to Bernadette's associates.

Morgan shook her head. "It would never have worked on Scarlett. She's too canny. And Wu and Vincenza don't handle paperwork. Jasmine put them away."

"Uh-oh."

Morgan worried a bitten cuticle with her teeth. She looked down at her nails. The polish had chipped already. *I bet Scarlett's polish wouldn't chip*, she thought. She shrugged. "I know. I hope she doesn't get in trouble."

"Why now?" Gabby rose, walking to the kitchen area to look out the window at the full moon. The fire escape cast shadows that darkened the room. "It's spooky out there."

"It all started with that stupid face cream."

"What stupid face cream?" Gabby asked absently. She held out her fingers, snapping for the licorice to float to her. Morgan looked at the candy, then moved her pointer finger casting a spell so the candy flew to Gabby. Gabby gloated as she caught it. "I'm really getting the hang of this."

"She's launching a new product with our DNA in it," Morgan announced.

"Ew."

"There's more to the story."

Gabby sat down cross-legged on the floor, her fishnet stockings torn at the knees. She looked intently at her friend. "Go on."

"This face cream will allow her to suggest things to anyone who wears it. She will be able to influence their thoughts."

"That's crazy. She can't do that. Anyway, that's impossible. How can you influence millions of people at one time?"

"Believe me, she's thought this through. She can, and she will."

"I thought she was a Davina. Davinas don't do that kind of stuff."

"Yeah, but she's acting like a Willa," Morgan said darkly.

"You have to stop her!" Gabby stood and started to pace.

"You don't understand. She's powerful. I mean, Oprah asks her for advice."

"You don't have a choice, Morgan. She's evil, like … like she probably wants to take over the world or something."

"I don't have the power to stop her. Oh, I can throw a wrench into her plans like the voting thing, but ultimately, she will win."

Gabby stopped, her face lighting up. "What are you talking about? We have something more powerful than any old spell." She grabbed her pink skull-and-crossbones shoulder bag and searched through it until she pulled out a micro USB. "Dahling, we'll go viral." She pressed the USB into Morgan's hand. "Together, we have enough followers on Twitter and Facebook to bury that bitch. Tomorrow you get the formula for the cream. We'll expose the ingredients. Every show will drop her ad. It will be like dumping a pail of water on her. She'll melt. Selfie! Let's post to Instagram." She plopped down next to her friend, her cell phone in her palm. "Smile!"

"That melting thing works only in the movies, by the way," Morgan told her sourly.

CHAPTER EIGHT

Wes stared dismally at the file, his face glum. The words swam before his tired eyes. He closed it with a snap and got up to grab a beer in the dimly lit kitchen. His apartment was small, on Steinway Street, over a souvlaki place that played Greek music day and night. The trill of the mandolins filled his space. The fan overhead circulated stale air. The smell of roasting meat from downstairs teased him. It was oppressively hot in his apartment.

His parents had a place on Long Island, surrounded by trees that was cool in the summer and warm in the winter. When he took his first apartment in Queens, he had been shocked by the stuffy rooms. But as much as he missed the island, he loved the busy streets with the ethnically diverse, open-air cafés.

After he graduated, he had backpacked through Europe, and Queens reminded him of Greece. He remembered visiting Delphi and learning about the Sibyls. Wise women had stood over a fissure which released toxic gases that were said to turn them into oracles that foretold events. A reasonable explanation for something that appeared mystical. Legends of their prophetic powers made them sought after by leaders around the world.

So, could they be regarded as witches too? he wondered.

Wes had learned about the witch hunts of the 15th and 16th centuries in school when he was a kid as well. Midwives and medicine women—or cunning women, as they were called —were often persecuted because people didn't understand the science of healing. The term *witch hunt* alone stirred up the concept of persecution. All they did was heal the sick or deliver babies. Science, he reasoned, explained the events taking place, but try as he might, he could not find science or even logic in the Witches Protection Program.

He leaned out the window, gazing at the large face of the moon, his mind swirling with thoughts of oracles, face cream, the girl, Alastair, and the idea of witches. *Well, at least it wasn't quite a full moon,* he thought. Much less spooky, the waning moon. Hopefully by the time he finished this assignment, there would be no moon, and all this nonsense would be a memory. He turned to his small kitchen. Junie's leftovers glowed gently with a pulsing green light. He should throw that crap out.

The biggest surprise was his father's knowledge of the program. Wes picked up the landline to call him. He punched in half the number and then put his finger on the disconnect button, hanging up. He felt his throat clog, not knowing where to start. He had questions—so many questions—but more than that, he wasn't sure he wanted to hear his father's answers.

He held one of his new business cards in his hand, turning it over. He folded it and then watched it flutter to the pavement below. His new badge lay discarded on the table next to the pop gun Alastair had issued him. He picked the badge up by the chain, swinging it around his wrist. The cool beads of the metal slapped his arm, winding tight. Then, he unraveled it faster and faster. Finally, he held it up, staring at the inane image of crossed witches' brooms. He caught the shield in his hand, then threw it against the wall, where bounced and landed near his shoes. He sat on his couch—a Danish modern salvaged from his folks' basement, and put his feet up, his head resting on a pillow.

Witches, he ruminated. *I mean, could it be possible?* He thought about Genevieve Fox. She was a sweet little lady, as tall as she was round, with a happy smile and wrinkled, blue-veined hands. She seemed harmless, with her soft chuckles and polite requests; he was sure he had gotten the instructions wrong.

It was his first assignment, in the backside of Nevada, the armpit of the country. A jail in a dry desert town in the middle of nowhere had her in an underground lockup. He and three others were supposed to transport her to L.A. An easy job, with simple instructions. She was a little old lady, for Christ's sake.

"Don't look at her eyes. Don't listen to her talk," his superior had informed him. They'd put a burlap bag over her head. It was medieval, gothic. Who put bags over people's heads?

Wes had shrugged as he led her into the school bus they were using for transport. He was advised to tie her up, all the way in the rear. He'd held her elbow as she shuffled, her swollen feet manacled together. She was so polite, her voice a frail thread when she asked for water. It was absurd. What was she? A drug lord? Terrorist? Gunrunner? He'd asked his fellow guard. It was an easy assignment, his father had assured him. *Don't screw it up.* He had pointed his fingers right at Wes's face. *Make me proud.*

Wes felt his eyes sting. His chest ached. He pressed a hand to his breastbone, feeling heat welling up in his chest cavity. He breathed out, fighting the strange feeling. Well, he hadn't made his dad proud. Closing his eyes, he tried to remember what had happened, but he came up with nothing. Nothing at all.

He left the room, falling exhausted onto his bed. Greenish shades of light from Junie's container bathed his apartment.

CHAPTER NINE

Y ou scared her off yesterday," Wes said crankily to his
nauseatingly cheerful partner.

"Maybe she got frightened when she saw two hundred and
fifty pounds of flesh barreling toward her. She's just a little itty-
bitty thing," Alastair said smugly.

"I'm not two hundred and fifty pounds, and I did not come
barreling toward her," Wes retorted. "Itty-bitty? Who are you?"

"A man with more years' experience finding witches than
you've lived on earth. Besides, I didn't get myself escorted out of
the building by two goons."

"I made it into the building."

"For what purpose?" Alastair replied. "Don't you think
anybody could have done that?"

Wes steamed with resentment. At the very least, he'd gotten
an idea of who they were up against, didn't he?

"Do you think I don't have an intimate knowledge of our
adversary?" Alastair said, as if reading Wes's thoughts.

"What's that got to do with your lack of understanding on

how to handle a possible lead? You totally blew that one," Wes growled back.

"And you didn't? I bet she burned that card to ashes when she got home."

Wes rubbed the spot under his breastbone that still tingled. He squirmed uncomfortably.

"What's the matter?" Alastair peered at him closely.

"Nothing. I don't know. Heartburn. There she is." Wes dashed out of the car before Alastair had a chance to react.

Morgan popped the rest of her sesame bagel into her mouth, her eyes scanning Sixth Avenue. It was early morning. Little gray sparrows fought for territory with the pigeons pecking at the crumbs beside the cart on the corner. The vendor held up a steaming Styrofoam cup of coffee, which she declined. A black SUV with dark windows slowed as it passed her. The window opened, and she made eye contact with the silver-haired man who had followed her yesterday. He slid the SUV into a space, and the younger blond man was out of the truck before she could move. He sprinted toward her, coming so close she could smell the clean scent of his aftershave. He clasped her wrist in a gentle hold, imprisoning her.

"We're not what you think." His deep voice was close to her ear, making her shiver. He held onto her, and while he knew that he was doing the same thing he'd accused his partner, his gut told him she didn't feel threatened.

The world narrowed to the two of them. She noticed his blue eyes seemed even brighter than she remembered. She looked up at him, observing wrinkles in the corners when he squinted in the sunlight. It made him look experienced, as if he had seen a lot in his lifetime. Much as she fought it, she found herself warming to his gentle smile.

"What do you know what I think? Let go of me." Morgan gave a halfhearted tug of her arm.

"We won't hurt you."

Morgan pulled away, but he held firm, so she dragged him toward a courtyard on the corner of the street as if she were the one holding onto him. They looked like a couple, and a woman looked up, smiling at them. There were concrete benches filled with people eating breakfast, texting, or enjoying the spring weather.

"I need to talk to you," he told her.

"You a fed?" She eyed him warily.

Wes thought for a minute on how to answer that, but before he could respond, the dark-haired girl blurted, "You work for my aunt."

He studied the distrust in her obsidian eyes. He wanted to reassure her. She had the look of someone who was lost. She glanced up and down the street nervously. He realized she was afraid, like the receptionist yesterday. He felt the need to make her feel safe. "No, I'm not a fed. We protect ... we protect people who are at risk."

"I'm not at risk," Morgan answered defiantly. "Look, I didn't ask for help. I don't even know who you are. The little guy"—she gestured at the truck window where Alastair sat watching them— "creeps me out."

Wes wanted to say me too, but he replied with, "We know your aunt is involved with something big. You don't want to be associated with it."

Morgan backed away from him, her expression wary. "You don't know me, and I don't want to know anything about you. Stay away from me."

"What do you know about the face cream?" Something flickered in her eyes, and Wes saw her waver with uncertainty. Her small body hummed with tension. "We could help you."

"I—I don't need anything."

Wes grabbed her hand, his grip warm and reassuring. He squeezed her fingers, a frisson of electricity startling them both. Morgan pulled her hand away, but he reached forward to touch her shoulder. She ducked away but looked up at him, her eyes softening.

"If you ever need help or you want to talk, you have my card."

Morgan cleared her throat. "No. I mean, I don't have it. Not anymore."

Wes pulled out another card, pressing it into her palm. Turning, he walked quickly back to the vehicle. Morgan watched as it was absorbed into traffic. She looked down at the card. The name Wesley Rockville and his number were printed on it, nothing else. "Wesley." Her lips formed his name soundlessly. "Wesley." This time, when she put his card in her bag, she did not crumple it up.

Squaring her shoulders, she walked into the building. Morgan ducked into a bathroom on the lobby level. She closed the door of the first stall, pulled out her wand, and held it high over her head, whispering, "Demons and witches hate Scarlett's strut. Let me be, just for a while, that blowsy, pathetic slut."

Morgan felt her legs stretch and shoulders widen, and she watched with fascinated interest as her hair lengthened, changing from dark to light. Cat-shaped eyes observed the new body. Morgan bit back a giggle. She had never morphed before. It felt … strange. She enjoyed the moment, almost wishing her aunt could see the successful spell. Shapeshifting was easier than she had thought. She walked around, looking at her unfamiliar hands and feet. Posing before the mirror, she practiced the sexy smile that Scarlett used. She took a deep breath, her eyes widening as huge breasts filled the tight shirt. She slid the wand up her sleeve, where she could feel it reassuringly against her wrist. Some liked using the wand, and others didn't. She was one who did.

Witches were known to have familiars, animals that helped do their bidding. Aunt Bea hated pets and refused to let Morgan have one, except for a lone goldfish that didn't last very long. Besides, Leo, as she called him, couldn't do much from the small, clear bowl he occupied. Every witch had a style exclusive to her territory and needs. Scarlett harnessed nature. Her aunt played an awful lot with her three stones, but Morgan had never caught her actually doing magic. She knew Bea used a family book with her favorite surefire spells. Morgan preferred to make it up as she went along.

Morgan stared at the strange reflection. She reached into her bag, taking out a tube of Pendragon matte red lipstick, and leaned forward to apply it generously to her newly plumped lips. She blotted her mouth, primped the blonde locks cascading onto her shoulders, and, turning sideways, admired Scarlett's boobs. They were enormous. *Maybe I'll keep the boobs,* she thought.

The door opened, and Morgan recognized Wu Chan Tsu, the Asian purchasing agent who worked closely in her aunt's inner circle. The long-standing enmity between Scarlett and Wu was known throughout the company. It had started over a man and ended with a legendary fight during one of the company picnics. Scarlett hated Wu, and Wu returned the favor. Wu was all tensile strength and coiled muscle compared with Scarlett's icy, womanly softness. Morgan always thought that Scarlett matched Wu's cruel coldness with her equally dark heart. Wu was beautiful, though, tall and slender, with straight black hair, and sloe eyes so black, they appeared devoid of light. Wu always dressed in dark leather. Morgan knew that she was some sort of specialist in martial arts as well. Morgan held her breath, worried Wu would sniff out her masquerade.

Wu pulled out mascara and touched up her soulless eyes. She looked sideways at the woman she assumed to be Scarlett and nodded coldly.

Morgan cleared her throat, hoping she'd sound like the assistant. "New wand?" she asked as she gestured at the mascara brush.

"Ha, very funny. I don't use willow wands," she said dismissively. "Did you finish the spreadsheets for me? La Bernadette is being a rare bitch."

Morgan replied that she had.

"Well, I didn't get them, Red. You better have them on my desk by one."

Clearly, Wu had a bit of an attitude this morning. Scarlett wouldn't let her talk down to her. *What would Scarlett do? What would she do?* Morgan racked her brain. Swallowing, she replied, her voice as cold as ice, "I'll get them there when I get them there. Deal with it."

"You're such a—"

"A what, Wu?" Morgan taunted. "Don't forget, I answer directly to Bernadette, and she doesn't take kindly to disrespect."

Wu turned to lean on the sink, coming face-to-face with Morgan. "High and mighty today, aren't we? You aren't the only one with influence." Wu's eyes narrowed to slits. She had elegant hands that ended with long, graceful nails. She swirled them in the air, creating an eddy of wind that ruffled Morgan's hair.

Morgan reached out, grabbing Wu's hand in a viselike grip. "Don't toy with me, and don't use magic." She squeezed hard, feeling one of Wu's nails break. Wu struggled to break free, but Morgan maintained the upper hand. They stood nose to nose, hatred emanating from them. She heard Wu's quick intake of breath and let her snatch her hand away.

"I won't forget this, Red."

Morgan sniffed. "Don't call me Red." She turned to leave the bathroom.

"This isn't over, Scarlett," Wu called after her.

Morgan laughed as she exited the bathroom, thinking payback was going to be a bitch for Scarlett.

Morgan grinned with surprise when Scarlett's eye recognition allowed her into the data center. The room was a large office filled with rows of computers containing all the information that made up Pendragon Cosmetics. Passing a server hotel, she found a lone station, then slid the USB into the port. Files raced down the screen. Morgan typed in the code for development, watching for the information that held the keys to the formula. Sweat beaded her brow. She brushed impatiently at the unfamiliar blonde hair that kept falling into her eyes. Scanning the data, she sighed with relief when the files for Pendragon Glow filled the screen. "Eureka," she whispered. She texted Gabby telling her she was on the way.

Outside, the corridors were busy with employees heading to their destinations. Wu walked back toward her office and encountered the real Scarlett outside her office.

"What are you doing here?" Wu demanded angrily.

Scarlett studied her colleague's tense face. "What's got your panties in a knot?" she asked, holding a thick folder of files.

Wu smashed her fist onto the folder. The papers scattered all over the floor.

"What's your problem?" Scarlett demanded, her fair face turning red with fury as the papers scattered around her.

"You dare to ask?" Wu spat. "Look—look what you did to me." She held out her abused finger, the nail broken to the quick. It happened to be her middle finger. Wu smirked at the message. "Read between the lines, Red."

Scarlett grabbed her hand, pushing it down. "What are you talking about?"

Wu snatched it away. "You broke my nail."

"Are you crazy? I never touched you."

Wu leaned over Scarlett, her eyes blazing. "You forgot what happened in the bathroom?"

"I don't know what you're talking about."

"You threatened me. In the bathroom."

"I haven't been out of Bernadette's office all morning. I don't know … What do you mean, we were in the bathroom together? Now?"

"Twenty minutes ago."

"If it wasn't me …" Scarlett took off. "Call the guards and have them check the cameras."

"What should I have them look for?"

"Tell them to look for me!" Scarlett yelled as she raced down the hallway.

Scant seconds later, Scarlett called Bernadette's private line. "There's been a breach."

"What are you talking about?" Bernadette asked impatiently.

"Someone's been in the data center. I'm heading down there." Scarlett watched her impersonator pull the USB from the computer. "Rudy," she said over the intercom, "there's someone pretending to be me in the data center. Detain her."

Morgan slid the USB into her bra as she walked briskly toward the door. Rudy Sinclair, a bespectacled security guard, opened the door, surprising her. She knew Rudy, had played at his station when she was a little girl. He grabbed her arm.

Morgan struggled with him. "What's the meaning of this? Bernadette sent me here—"

"I don't know who you are, but I know you are not Scarlett LoPretti."

"Let go of me." Morgan felt her magic slipping as she morphed back into herself. She shrank as she felt the spell end.. Rudy's hold slipped away.

Rudy reared back in shock. "Miss Pendragon?" What … how?" His face was shocked. "I'm sorry."

Scarlett's voice broke over the speaker in the room. "Bring her in, Rudy," she shouted angrily. "She's trespassing."

"I can't trespass at my own company!" Morgan shouted.

Clearly, Rudy was torn. Scarlett shouted again, "Bring her in, now!"

"I'm really sorry, miss, but I report to Miss LoPretti." He reached for her arm.

Morgan crouched down quickly, escaping his hold. Sliding her fingers along the dusty floor, then letting her wand fall into her ready hand, she spun, crying out, "Arise and fly, this you must, coat his glasses with lots of dust!"

The air filled with dirt, choking them both. Rudy was blinded by the thick layer of dust that covered the lenses of his glasses. Morgan raced out the door, coughing, the tornado of debris following her as she made a mad dash for the stairs. She pointed her humming wand at the exit door to the stairwell. "No time to waste, give me speed, slide down forty floors on my ass, indeed." Morgan lifted her backside so that it rode the bannister, the floors racing past her as she jumped from landing to landing. She repeated her spell until she appeared to be was a blurred smudge on the cameras.

Scarlett stood behind Bernadette, who was watching the fleeing image of her niece escaping the building.

"Is she flying?"

Bernadette made a negative sound that turned into a chuckle. "No, Morgan doesn't fly, but apparently she knows how to slide really fast." She shook her head. "Naughty Morgan, what are you up to?" She turned to Scarlett. "Get Wu and Vincenza on it. Bring her back." She looked at the younger woman's vicious expression. "Scarlett, I don't want her harmed."

Scarlett smiled, and Bernadette wondered what she found amusing.

Morgan sprinted through the lobby, darting between the milling crowd. She heard someone shout, "Shut down the front entrance!"

Alarms blared, startling the crowd of people so they went wild with fear. People made a mad dash for the exits, pushing others as they tried to escape the building. There was mass confusion.

Breathing hard, Morgan slipped and her feet slid out from under her on the polished marble floor. Pushing to her feet, she scrambled toward the revolving door, feeling it seize just as she felt the cool outside air hit her face. Half out, she squeezed through the opening, losing her jacket to the door. Her arm was scraped raw from wrist to elbow, but she was free. Breathing heavily, she looked about wildly to see if she was being followed.

"Here she comes," Alastair said patiently.

Wes turned to see Morgan struggling to thrust herself through the jammed revolving door. He unbuckled his seat belt.

"Where do you think you're going?" Alastair asked.

"I'm going to help her."

"Not so fast, Galahad," Alastair cautioned him.

"She's in trouble!" Wes started to leave the car, but Alastair's hand restrained him.

"She's got to come to us."

"They're never going to let her go. Look." Wes motioned to the groups of security rounding the block to intercept.

Morgan knew her pursuers were behind her. She raced out of the building, skirting through the crowds. Glancing back, she saw Wu and Vincenza in the lobby. Wu pointed, and they rushed the revolving door, pushing people out of the way. As they emerged, the two split up. Morgan looked back, panicking for a moment. Three guards were headed up the street from the opposite direction. She was trapped.

"Shit," Wes whispered. Watching the glass door, he felt chills erupt on his spine as two women burst through the entrance. One was Asian, the other very dark. Both wore black pantsuits. The air trembled before them. The Asian female wavered, then shimmered, transforming into a hawk. The other woman dropped to all fours, her movements feline, as a black panther leaped onto the sidewalk. People were shouting. It was chaos. Screams filled the air. Bystanders grappled with their cell phones, filming the hawk's giant wingspan and the panther's loping stride.

"Did you see what happened?" Wes yelled.

"Looks like a hostile work environment," Alastair replied, flooring the accelerator and propelling the SUV over the curb to jump in front of Morgan. "Crap! By the evening news, everybody is going to be talking about witches. Get in, Morgan!" Alastair shouted.

Wes jumped out, the hawk attacking his shoulders with its sharp beak. He grabbed Morgan's arm, lifting her off the pavement. The girl looked stunned. Wes turned at the sound of a growl in time to see the huge panther leap at him. Wes twisted and tried to haul Morgan into the SUV. He felt Alastair grab the girl, relieving him of his burden. He kicked the panther squarely in the face, feeling its teeth catch on his shoe as the big cat bit down. Wes cursed, feeling his shoe fill with blood. He grabbed Alastair's umbrella from where it rested in the front and hit the panther squarely on the head. The hawk shrieked loudly in his ear, its razor-sharp claws trying to grasp him from above. Wes pointed upward and pressed the lever. The umbrella sprang open, smacking the hawk so that it was propelled backward into an oncoming taxi's front hood. The cab careened across four lanes, horn blaring. The taxi plowed into a bus, bounced off, and landed on a fire hydrant, causing the hydrant to burst and release a geyser of water that would put Old Faithful to shame.

"Do something!" Morgan screamed, landing on the console between the two seats. Wes kicked at the panther, trying to dislodge its hold. Sirens blared. Wes heard a roar but wasn't sure if it was the animal or inside his head. The hawk was back, pounding the windshield until it was pocked with several spiderwebs of broken glass. There was a sonic blast; a stream of hot steam flew past him. Alastair held his strange-looking gun at the cat's head and let loose a steady fountain of a green, foamy liquid that forced the beast to release Wes's foot with a howl of pain. The panther fell on its backside and transformed into a swarthy woman with torn pants and blood dripping from her feral lips.

Wes landed in the truck, gasping, "Punch it!" He slammed the door. Morgan scrambled to the rear seat.

The hawk was spread-eagled across the windshield, its pointy beak chipping away at the glass.

"Put on the wipers!" Wes yelled. "That'll scrape it off!"

"I have something even better," yelled Alastair.

Alastair pushed the button, and to Wes's surprise, the wipers released the same foamy liquid as the gun. The hawk screamed as it relinquished its hold, falling to the side. Morgan glanced back to see Wu sprawled on the street, wiping the goo from her furious face.

Wes pointed to the shattered windshield. "What was that all about?"

"Shape-shifting," Alastair told him as he observed Morgan.

"Take me to Queens," Morgan demanded.

"What, do you think I'm Uber?" Alastair asked.

Morgan stared angrily out the window. "I don't care what you do. I'm not answering any questions."

Sirens blared as cop cars raced toward the building behind them. They moved toward the east side, the traffic thinning. Here and there, another cop car raced past them.

They slowed down. The danger had passed. Wes looked backward, confirming they weren't being followed. He looked at Morgan, her hair streaming in her face, her clothes in disarray. Her complexion drained of color.

"What were you doing that caused all that?" he asked.

Alastair watched the two younger people closely. He'd noticed the girl only had eyes for his partner. He stayed quiet.

"I didn't ask for your help," she told them rudely.

"You didn't have to," Wes responded hotly. "I don't know where those things came from, but they could have killed you."

Morgan swallowed hard, then shook her head. Alastair could see the gleam of unshed tears in her eyes. "No, they wouldn't. You don't know the first thing about them. They wanted something ... They just wanted to take something back from me. They would never hurt me."

Wes looked to Alastair for confirmation. The older man shrugged. He looked back at Morgan as if Alastair's doubt confirmed his own feelings. "It didn't look that way to me."

Morgan ignored him, staring angrily out the window.

"You're not going to let her go?" Wes demanded.

"Not right here and now, but as soon as we are safe, I will," Alastair told him.

"This makes no sense! She's in danger. They attacked me and would have torn her to ribbons if I hadn't stepped in the way."

"You can't protect a witch that doesn't want interference. Right, Morgan?" Alastair looked at her in the rearview mirror, their eyes meeting. "It's one of the tenets of their belief; it's based on freedom."

"I don't know what you are talking about." Morgan stared out the window.

"I know," Alastair said quietly, but his eyes never left the girl's face.

They approached the Fifty-ninth Street Bridge, easing between buses and sleek limousines. Morgan perked up. They were heading for Queens.

"Don't get too excited. We're not stopping there. This is to make sure we're not being followed." Alastair turned to Wes, who was examining his foot. "How bad?"

"Puncture wound. Do you think I need a rabies shot?"

"Nah," Alastair responded. "She was harmless, right, Morgan? You should see what Bernadette can do."

"My aunt doesn't shape-shift." She handed Wes a rag she

found on the back seat. Their fingers touched. A sizzle jumped from his fingertip to hers. Morgan pulled back her hand, noticing there was blood. She wiped it on the seat, but it didn't come off.

"Yeah," Wes said hotly. "I'll bet she's a Davina, too."

Morgan turned back to the window, ignoring him.

"We want to know about Pendragon Glow," Wes demanded. "You owe us that."

"Get in line at Wal-Mart," Morgan said flatly. While she didn't agree with her aunt, she would handle this on her own.

They stopped at a light. The car was silent, and the entrance to the bridge yawned before them. A cop lazily waved her arms, admitting the cars one at a time. Morgan sat up, feeling her back pocket for her phone. She gasped, searching her front pockets. It must have been in her jacket. The jacket caught by the revolving door.

"Lose something?" Wes asked calmly.

"None of your business."

Before he could respond, the back window was forcefully hit, causing the car to rock. The hawk had slammed its head against the glass and shattered it. Morgan screamed. Alastair looked for room to move forward fast, but there was none. The hawk continued to batter the back window, the sound of breaking glass filling the interior.

Wes turned with the rifle, screaming, "Get down!"

Morgan threw herself on the floor as a stream of the green liquid flew over her. Several drops leaked from the trigger, and Wes heard Morgan gasp as they plopped onto her shoulder, burning her shirt.

The hawk screamed and moved so its body hung over the rear window, away from the frothing weapon. Wes smelled the stench of burning feathers. He pressed on, half out of his seat, but the hawk was now above them, gripping the shattered window frame with its fierce talons.

Alastair pressed the accelerator, making the car jerk forward, then slammed hard on the brakes, forcing the hawk to lose its hold. It flew up and over the front of the truck, smashing into the policewoman, taking them both down to the pavement in a frenzy of smoking feathers. Alastair careened past them, taking the outer bridge crossing and making it across in record time. He pulled into a parking garage on the other side of the bridge, entering what seemed to be a black hole. They drove five levels down. Alastair moved the car into a space in the corner. Exiting, he looked back into the darkened interior, saying, "Well, come on. We haven't got all day."

"Where are we going?" Morgan asked, following him to a small four-door Fiat.

"I'm taking you home," Alastair told her.

Morgan shook her head. "It won't be safe. I'll find my way back on my own."

Wes held her arm, a frisson going through the two of them. He shook his head. "Come with us."

"No, no thanks," she said grudgingly. "I have a safe place. Take me to Ninth Avenue."

Alastair nodded, opening the door to the little black car. Wes watched Morgan get out of the vehicle. She moved to the front window, looking closely at them both. She opened her mouth to say something, then appeared to change her mind. Wes glanced at Alastair, and when he turned back to her, she was gone.

"This isn't police work. This isn't protection!" Wes shouted to Alastair.

"It certainly looks that way, but looks can be deceiving," Alastair said calmly. "Every journey takes you somewhere. You won't see your destination until you get there."

Wes shook his head, his foot throbbing like a sore tooth, and muttered, "First I'm a chew toy, and now I'm stuck with Gandalf and Yoda's prison child as a partner. Help."

"Indeed. I'm taking you to Bags to fix that foot of yours," Alastair told him.

Wes leaned his hot head against the window, wordlessly mouthing, "Help ..."

CHAPTER TEN

Bernadette stalked her office, Jasmine looking small in the chair opposite her. Scarlett walked in, her face tight. "They've lost her."

Bernadette spun, her face twisted. "How could you have let this happen?" She pointed to a monitor over the seating area. "Look, you idiot. I told you no shapeshifting! It's going to be all over the news."

Jasmine's tear-stained face turned up to the two women as she repeated, "Shapeshifting?" in a hushed tone.

Scarlett looked at her, sneering. "Oh, shut up." She turned to her seething boss. "I told them to be discreet!" she said defensively. "Don't blame me. Blame your precious niece; she's working with the feds."

"Morgan is not working with them," Bernadette told her firmly. "She wouldn't betray me."

"Yeah, sure," Scarlett responded. She looked at the quaking assistant with disdain. "She shouldn't be hearing any of this."

"Like it's going to make a difference now," Bernadette said, her gray eyes glued on the news broadcast of the images of animals attacking the SUV. "It looks like they missed the transition."

"It probably happened too fast. Nobody will believe the few who did see it."

"No thanks to you. I need just a few more weeks. Is that too much to ask? First Morgan, then Washington, now this ..." She sighed, sitting down. "And Jasmine, what am I going to do about you? Where did you put the papers I asked for?"

"I-I—" Jasmine stuttered.

"Out with it. Where are the papers Morgan signed?"

"She didn't," Jasmine blurted. "She was there, and then ... I don't know. She was gone, and so were the files. I'm so sorry, Bernadette."

"I detest tears, Jasmine," Bernadette said icily.

"Fire her." Scarlett shrugged.

"I put too much training into her."

Jasmine fearfully watched the two women talk about her as though she wasn't there.

"At this point, she knows too much," Scarlett offered. "You could kill her."

Jasmine's quick intake of breath alerted them to her attempt to rush for the door. Scarlett stopped her by raising her hand and squeezing her thumb and forefinger together. Energy shot from her fingertips to the girl, freezing her in her tracks. Jasmine rose off the floor, immobile and encased in a purple fog. Her eyes were closed, her face relaxed.

Bernadette looked up at her floating assistant, dismissing her. "Oh, go do something with her already," she told Scarlett. "Wipe her memory away. Make her as simple as she was before." She threw her a look of warning. "I want her in working condition, Scarlett. Nothing devastating."

"I'll give her something else to think about," Scarlett said silkily, touching the fine skin of Jasmine's face, "once I've sucked her memory dry."

Wu and Vincenza entered the office, interrupting the women. Vincenza was attracted to Scarlett and made no bones about it. Her smoky eyes took in Scarlett's lush figure, and she purred like the panther she had been not fifteen minutes ago.

Wu sneered, still blaming Scarlett for her broken nail.

"Where's my niece?" Bernadette demanded.

"She got away," Wu said through gritted teeth.

"You incompetent morons." Bernadette leaned over the desk, her face white with rage. "You shape-shifted in public!" She pointed to the screen with fury. "By tonight, this place will be crawling with police and FBI, and every other agency will be breathing down our necks. If you've jeopardized the release of this cream, I will send you both back to the two-bit villages you came from!"

Vincenza threw a cell phone onto the stone top of the table.

"We found this," Wu said with a triumphant sneer at Scarlett.

Bernadette picked up Morgan's phone, scrolling down the messages. "Who's this Gabby?"

Scarlett walked over. "Her best friend. Her only friend. Poor Morgan. Poor little witch girl," she taunted.

"I don't think you're funny. She says here that she's on her way." Bernadette tossed the phone to Wu, who caught it deftly. "Think you can bring her back?" she asked snidely.

"I may have to shape-shift."

Bernadette nodded; her face closed. "Be discreet. Don't screw it up this time." With a wave, she dismissed her, then turned her gimlet eye on Scarlett. "You're still here?" She looked at Jasmine, considering her. "She has such pretty skin. Do something that will keep her occupied, so she won't be thinking about what happened tonight."

Scarlett nodded as she walked toward the exit. "Lovely skin, gone on a whim, and in its place, a pus-filled crater face." She added as she left the room, "When you wake, we'll commiserate, and in the end, you'll see me as your only friend."

Bernadette smiled. She could trust Scarlett. She always followed orders.

She held out a paper for Vincenza. "Go to public relations. I want a story of a photo shoot gone awry. Hire a bird and a cat."

Vincenza growled, earning her a tight-lipped look from her boss. "Stop it already. It may be fun for you, but the cleanup is a bitch. I don't want to keep having these issues." Vincenza slipped soundlessly from the room.

Bernadette sat down, drained. Picking up the middle stone, she laid it on her chest, feeling the heat radiate into her cold heart. With a heavy sigh, she pulled out the ancient book from her bottom drawer. It had a metal clasp that fell open with a touch of her finger. Wetting her pointer finger, she fluttered through the fragile parchment. Her lips moved rapidly, and she made a sound of disapproval. Holding her finger in that spot, she turned a few more pages, smiling with satisfaction. Her whispered words were fast, and in a language not many could comprehend. Satisfied, she picked up the phone, took a deep breath, and punched in a number. "There's been a problem," she said softly to the person on the other end. Her gray eyes never left the book.

Scarlett walked out of the office. Jasmine floated after her, her smooth, caramel skin breaking out in ulcerated pockmarks. Jasmine carried on, unaware of her changing appearance. Scarlett watched the other two women enter the outer elevators to search for Morgan. Twirling her blonde locks, she whispered, "Make Morgan disappear, I don't care, so that I'm the one and only—Bernadette's heir." Snickering, she snapped her fingers, bringing Jasmine back to herself.

"Whew," Jasmine smiled, "that was close. Thanks for saving my job."

CHAPTER ELEVEN

"I said, come on," Alastair urged the younger man.

"I want to go to a hospital." They stood in the claustrophobic hallway, Wes's bloody foot leaving a trail of red footprints.

Alastair shook his head. "What are you afraid of? Witches are synonymous with healers. Bags is practically a surgeon."

"What do you mean, *practically?*" Wes roared. "I'm not going in." He limped after Alastair, who stood firm.

"Shapeshifting witches sometimes release slow-acting hormones that can enter the bloodstream and wreak havoc on a person's nervous system. It starts with an elevated temperature."

Wes felt sweat drip from his temple down his warm neck. His body shook with a tremor.

"You're looking a little flushed there." Alastair reached up to press his cool hand against Wes's overheated cheek. He *tsk*ed. Wes pulled away. "Listen, conventional medicine doesn't have a clue …"

"All right, already," Wes said, giving in. He felt lightheaded. "I don't know if I trust her."

"Do you trust *me*?" Alastair asked, his eyes boring into Wes's. The younger man looked away.

He was still protesting after Junie had placed his foot on a dish towel on her lime velvet couch. She ignored his complaints as she poked around the hole oozing blood, which she collected into a porcelain cup. "For later," she advised Alastair, who nodded sagely. "Nothing like fresh blood."

"Fresh blood. Alastair, get me out of here!" Wes wailed.

Luna pounced on his chest and walked down to his injured foot to look at the wound. She meowed loudly.

Junie looked up, her bulbous eyes grossly enlarged by the thick glasses she wore. "I know. It does look Italian," she commented back.

"Italian, you say?" Alastair bent over to observe.

"Mmm, see the teeth marks? These particular panthers come from the hills over Catanzaro."

"Catanzaro … I thought they only bred cougars," Alastair commented.

"Only the old ladies hunting young men in the bars." Junie laughed. "No, no, this is definitely a panther bite. There's a coven that roams the area. Nasty women, famous for their hot tempers."

Wes drifted, despite the conversation. Junie patted his rear, advising him that this was going to sting a bit.

Hot needles stung his foot from toe to ankle as a boiling towel was placed on his abused limb. Wes reared up off the couch, only to have strong hands hold him back. A rainbow of colors danced before his closed eyes before they rolled back in his head.

"He's out," Alastair told Junie.

"I can tell from his aura," she replied as she cleaned his wounds. "Better this way."

"He didn't want to come. I told him some taradiddle about

panther hormones." Alastair held up a lamp for her to see better.

"Good. It's more believable than the truth." Junie sliced open his foot, squeezing out the poison. "A few more hours, and he'd be dead meat." She stood back, cracking her back, satisfied with her handiwork. Together they removed his shirt, then Junie dabbed the scratches on his shoulders. "Hmmm ... nasty piece of work here." She threw a fuzzy knitted blanket over him.

"How long till he wakes?"

Junie walked back into her tiny kitchen to return holding a lacy curtain of caul fat from a midsize animal. It was draped over her hands and smelled like rotten meat. "Keep his foot elevated."

"Sheep?" Alastair asked.

"Goat." Junie shrugged. "I read his leaves and I got goats."

"Who'd have thunk it?" Alastair laughed.

Junie wrapped his foot with the thoughtful competency of a practiced nurse. "Don't laugh. I don't make these things up, I only treat." She grabbed her willow branch from a side table and, bowing her head, hummed loudly. Alastair hastily moved to the other side of the room.

"I don't want it touching me," he told her.

"This ain't my first rodeo." She cleared her throat loudly. "Maaaaake him beeeetter, maaake it heeeeeal." She sounded like a nanny goat and Alastair bit back a smile.

"Meeeelt the faaaaat, into his heeeel. Faaaaaster, faaaaaaster and on this note, maaaaake the paaaanther lose to a gooooat."

An eerie blue light surrounded Wes. The animal fat sizzled on his foot. The room smelled like a Sunday barbecue. It turned to liquid as it dissolved into his skin.

"Well," Junie said as she put down her wand, "that should do it. Coffee?"

"I need to see if anything made the news."

Junie nodded, indicating Alastair should follow her. "I've got a small TV in the kitchen."

"So, how long will he sleep?"

"Half hour, maybe an hour, and he'll be kicking his heels in no time."

Both Alastair's and Junie's chuckles floated through the apartment to merge with Wes's disturbing dreams. He roused from the noise, then let himself be sucked into the strange, mountainous world he had entered. He was high on a hill, the wind blowing harshly, stinging his eyes. He climbed higher, and higher, but he couldn't figure out why.

Junie pointed the remote, and the television lit up with the evening news. Alastair's face turned grim when the screen filled with his SUV racing down the street, the hawk plastered against his windshield.

The newscaster stated, "The question of the day is, who let the dogs out? Or the panther and hawk? At two o'clock this afternoon, a panther mysteriously appeared to chase this Escalade, then strangely disappeared at the same time this gray hawk attacked the SUV while it traveled down the Avenue of the Americas. No one has claimed the wild cat, and the hawk cannot be traced either. Tony Arrolos found out that onlookers say they came out of nowhere."

The screen changed to the city street. A reporter in the crowd held his out microphone for an eyewitness.

"Can you tell us what you saw?"

The bystander shook her head. "They appeared out of thin air and just attacked that SUV. It wasn't as big as a panther. It couldn't be one. I think it was an oversized cat. You know, a wild one. It had a man by the foot, but the SUV took off so quickly, I thought I imagined the whole thing."

"Yeah," a man in painter overalls added. "It looked like they

hit a lady in the street. I tried to help her, but she ran in there."
He pointed to the Pendragon building. "She looked stunned.
Had some blood on her cheek."

"Did you see where the cat went?"

Another woman pointed to an alleyway across the street. "It
ran away. It was afraid of the hawk. It was trying to protect the
man."

"There you have it, folks. Three versions of one scene. All
we know is the SUV took off with the hawk on the windshield
and animal control has not seen either animal. Commissioner
Bannor has stepped up patrols in the area and asks that the
public report any strays. This is Tony Arrolos, reporting live
from Manhattan."

Junie looked at Alastair. "They don't realize they are
witches."

"Yet," Alastair said ominously.

CHAPTER TWELVE

Morgan changed into one of Gabby's tees. It swam on her, but it was clean. She disinfected the scrape on her forearm, then dabbed her shoulder with antiseptic, her eyes watering from the burn.

"Ugh," Gabby commented, handing her a clean towel. "Is that blood yours?"

"No." Morgan shook her head. Some of Wes's blood stained her hands. She had handed him a rag, and when he touched her hand, he must have gotten blood on her. She remembered because there had been a distinct spark between them when their hands met. The bottom of the yellowed porcelain sink turned pink, but her fingers wouldn't come clean. Morgan scrubbed hard, her skin turning pink from her ministrations.

"Did you get it?" Gabby asked. "Try this." She poured a clear liquid from a brown bottle over Morgan's hands. Morgan reared back, her palms on fire.

"What is that?" she screamed, her eyes watering.

Gabby looked at the label. "Witch hazel." She turned on cold water and held her friend's burning fingers under the stream. They watched with stunned fascination as the blood was absorbed into the injured skin. "Oops," Gabby said quietly. "I know what will make you feel better. Let's get you something to eat, and then we'll upload the information and watch the crap hit the fan."

"Where are you uploading it?" Morgan asked as she flopped down on the couch. She was staring at her hands, not liking the tingling sensation. She rubbed them on the couch but felt no relief. "Lucky Charms!" Morgan shouted with glee. Gabby placed a cracked bowl and a container of milk on the coffee table.

"They're magically delicious," Gabby replied. "We are going to inform the twenty-two thousand followers on my blog, my eight hundred thousand Twitter followers, Facebook, Instagram, my website ... all about Auntie Bea's weird cosmetic ingredients."

Morgan reached into her bra, taking out the USB with the stolen information.

"Ooh la la," Gabby said, snatching the device and plugging it into the port on her laptop.

"Won't be long and Aunt Bea will have to reconsider her product line." She turned to look at Morgan, her blue eyes appealing. "Maybe you'll run the company."

"I don't mind Bea. I just don't like her methods. She has been a strict parent to me—"

"More like a commandant," Gabby interrupted.

"But still a parent. Yay," Morgan said, changing the subject, her mouth filled with dissolving marshmallows. "I love this stuff." She hated talking crap about Bea. Despite her controlling ways, Morgan loved her aunt. She was the only parent she'd ever known.

"I got plenty more where that came from," Gabby informed her. "Time for a celebration. I went shopping today."

"What's on the menu?"

"Gummy worms, gummy bats ..."

"I love those," Morgan crooned.

"Licorice spiders, and we'll wash it down with a BK Oreo Milkshake."

"Where's the protein?"

"I said bats."

"You're wicked," Morgan told her with a grin.

"I'm trying." Gabby smiled back. "We'll go back to salads tomorrow. Tonight, we feast!"

CHAPTER THIRTEEN

W es felt a chill dance down his spine, pulling him out of his slumber with an abrupt start. A solid weight held him down. For a minute, he panicked, until a low meow informed him of his oppressor. He sat up, pushing both Luna and the shabby crocheted blanket from his chest. He was naked from the waist up. He touched a healed scratch on his shoulder. Gingerly, he placed his foot on the floor, marveling that the pain was gone. It felt greasy and smelled like the souvlaki joint that operated under his apartment.

He heard the sound of a television coming from the kitchen. He rose to his feet unsteadily, walking drunkenly toward the noise. His foot had the sensation as if it was asleep. He stamped it, wincing with pain as his blood rushed through it.

Alastair and Junie were sitting at the table, a steaming cup before each and a half-eaten marble cake on a plate. Wes felt his mouth water, and his stomach rumbled noisily.

"I love a man with an appetite." Junie stood. "I have some stew on."

"No stew!" Wes told her loudly.

He weaved a bit. Alastair pushed him into the chrome chair. He looked up at the black-and-white television. *Black and white?* he thought.

Alastair pointed. "We were watching the latest report. They're saying the animals escaped from a photo shoot for a commercial they were doing in the Pendragon building."

"Those weren't animals!" Wes shook his head.

"As far as the public knows and is willing to admit, they were. People look for the most reasonable explanation."

"So, witches are not public as of yet," Wes said, turning to look out the window. Luna purred contently and jumped on his lap. He considered the moon. It was waning just a bit more tonight. Another week or two to a new moon phase and his plan was to be out of this program. An owl hooted; he wondered where owls found a home in Brooklyn under the elevated train. A shiver made his whole body convulse, though he wasn't cold. Wispy clouds moved across the sky, covering the face of the moon, making Wes feel smothered. He cleared his throat, a sense of unease creeping over him. His insides felt jittery. The only person he could think of was Morgan. The owl hooted again, this time with a response from another bird.

Junie came up behind him, her head cocked.

"Alastair," she whispered. "Did you hear that? I have to get out of here. Now."

Wes turned to face the other man, his face filled with astonishment. "Morgan's in trouble." He couldn't explain how he knew it, but he did.

"I know," Alastair said quietly, looking into his eyes. "We can't wait any longer."

Wes wondered how he knew and why he was so sure of it. "Do you know where she is?" The cat leaped from his arms.

"She hasn't left her friend's place." Alastair held out his shirt. "I have someone watching."

The old woman ran to the kitchen. Wes heard her slopping that stupid stew into a fast-food container.

"Leave it," Alastair called.

Junie ignored him. She stuffed it into a bag she pulled from under the table. Looking into the depths of her old mirror, she said, "Sorry, old friend. I'll be back for you."

Wes watched, wide-eyed, as the mirror brightened, then went dark.

Alastair silently shut off the lights. In a minute, they were gone.

CHAPTER FOURTEEN

G abby waltzed into the kitchen to open the refrigerator door. Buttery light bathed her freckled face. She hummed a song, searching through soggy Chinese takeout containers and rolled-up balls of wax papers holding bits of leftover sandwiches. "No, no, no ... *yesss.*" She found the milkshake, took a long sip, and shivered with delight. "We have to share. I only have one," she called back to her friend.

Her slim back to the window, Gabby failed to see the flapping wings settling down to morph into the dark shape of Wu.

Crouching down, Wu peered through the glass, her eyes flitting around to take in the contents of the shabby room. *Not much to work with,* she thought with a sneer. There was a small Formica table filled with candy, gummy insects spilled all over its surface. Wu considered the mess. *Be discreet,* Bernadette had ordered. She could kill the redhead, the wannabe witch. Wu considered the option but remembered Bernadette's warning. "I'll get you another day," Wu whispered to the girl who thought she was a witch, the pretender. She needed to get Morgan out to where she could scoop her up from the street.

She had to find a way to separate her from the safety of her friend. The girl and the gummies. She frowned. *Not much to work with.*

"Time for you to listen to me, do my bidding like a robotic zombie," Wu murmured as she flapped her arms, watching in satisfaction as Gabby dropped the shake, her hands lifeless at her sides. The girl spun to look out the window, her eyes yellow blazes of light. Wu turned her attention to the candies on the table. Moving her fingers in swirling motions, she chuckled, watching the outcome of her spell.

"Spiders, worms, and bats can swarm; to that, Morgan will run outside with alarm."

The tabletop became a swarming mess of black, red, and orange nature herself could not reproduce if she tried. Tiny bats squeaked, flying en masse around the cramped kitchen. They landed on the girl, who held out floppy arms. Gummy spiders created lacy, gummy webs. The worms and spiders used them to march onto the girl, covering her skin with crawling bugs.

"Gab," Morgan called. "Where's my shake?"

Wu raised two fingertips, making a walking motion. The redhead robotically made her way into the next room, bugs covering her, a nest of gummy bats in her red hair.

Morgan sat on the floor, the laptop before her. She had the USB in her hand and was examining it. "Hey, Gab," she said without turning around. "Something's wrong. It's not loading. Gab?" Morgan slowly looked up, her eyes widening with fear. Her friend was covered with squirming insects, their sticky residue turning her fair skin dark. She stood, knocking over the computer, the USB forgotten in her hand, her mouth opening in a silent scream. She hated spiders. Morgan could face anything but spiders. She had a primal fear of the little beasties. Her heart jumping in her throat, she inched backward as Gabby pushed toward her, her face devoid of expression, her eyes a fierce yellow.

Her bag was across the room, her wand hidden in its dark depths. Picking up a pencil, she waved it frantically at her friend. "Candy is dandy; stay sweet, and turn back into a treat," she said in a rush to no avail. Morgan moaned, trying something else. "Sugar melt quick as ice; candy should always behave nice." Nothing. The candy and her friend were moving like a solid wall of gelatinous critters. "Bad magic, go away. Turn back to candy, come what may!" Morgan cursed loudly as she backed away, slipping on a gummy spider. Bats pulled at Gabby's hair, fluttering toward Morgan, their gummy wings ripping strands right off her friend's oblivious head. Shooting cobwebs reached for Morgan, snagging themselves on her T-shirt. She brushed them, her hands sticky, her face stark with horror. Morgan looked wildly around. "Bea, let her go!" she screamed. "Stop it! Please, Aunt Bea." A worm made the leap, landing with a plop on her forehead. Morgan screamed again, clawing at the slimy crawler.

Wu watched with amusement from her perch on the window, smiling humorlessly. Spiders attached themselves to Morgan's arms. Her flesh was glued to the things. Morgan sobbed helplessly, turning when the door splintered. The blond man from the truck stepped through the wreckage. He took one look at Gabby and flicked a Darrow Trance Lifter from his pocket, enveloping Gabby in a blue haze.

The light surrounded Gabby, forcing her to convulse. Her yellow eyes turned white then rolled back in her head. Wes held out his weapon, the laser beam aimed for the middle of her candy-encrusted torso. He tucked it back into his pocket, his strong arms grabbing Morgan, brushing the creepy crawlers until they fell from her body. A warm jacket surrounded her. Morgan sighed with relief. She recognized the tangy scent of a familiar aftershave—the cop, what was his name? Presley ... Wesley ... Wesley Rockville had her in a solid embrace. *Rock solid,* Morgan thought hazily.

"We have to get out of here." His muffled words vibrated. Morgan felt safe.

"Gabby?" she asked breathlessly.

"Help is on the way."

"My bag. Grab my bag."

Wes spied the hobo bag on the floor, covered with melted candy. Brushing it off, he tucked it under his arm. "Got it!" Wes told her as he whisked her out of the room.

Wu smashed the window as she watched her spell dissolve. "No, no, no!" she screamed.

"Ni hao! You yige meihow de yewan, ni feng kuang de nuwu?" Alastair said, greeting the witch and asking in perfect Mandarin whether the crazed sorceress was having a nice evening. He stood in the alley, looking up at her on the fire escape.

Wu spun, cursing right back at him in Chinese.

"That's not nice!" Alastair said. His hands were in his pockets. He appeared casual, like a person out for a stroll.

Wu glared at him and then at her Harley parked at the end of the dark alley. Raising her arms over her head she pointed a finger toward her motorcycle, cast a spell, lifting it twenty feet in the air, let it hover, and then threw it at his head. Alastair deftly stepped aside, watching with amused interest as it landed in a smoking heap.

"Now, how do you expect to get home, Wu? Fly?"

Wu shrieked, opening her arms wide, her dark body transforming into feathers, her face the beady visage of a hawk. The scream echoed eerily down the dark streets, bouncing off the closely packed buildings, as though another bird answered.

"I know you're alone," Alastair shouted. He peered through

the darkness, nodding to Wes, who was running toward the car, Morgan in his arms. "Get out of here," he called to him.

Wes looked back, shaking his head. "I'll be right there."

"I plan on ruffling her feathers. I got this," Alastair said confidently. He looked up at Wu. "Why don't you come down so we can do this with a minimal amount of damage?"

Wu circled high above him, her eyes bright pinpoints of light. She widened her route. Her face turned to Wes and Morgan.

"Don't even think about it, Wu. You're not going to make it," Alastair called.

The hawk shrieked loudly, feinted left, but dove right.

"Bad bird!" Alastair called out as he reached into his trench coat, snapping a metal lasso attached to the end of his Steampunk gun. The thick chain arced up with a crack and, with a snake-like movement, flickered near Wu's face. Wu lifted up, changing direction, and dove at him, her wings spread as wide as a small plane. Alastair ran toward a dumpster, squeezing behind it. The hawk came out of her descent, speeding upward and landing on a fire escape. Her intense gaze peered through the darkness, waiting for Alastair's next move.

Alastair inched out, holding his lasso tightly looped in his capable hands. His eyes found the bird, just out of his reach. The two adversaries measured each other. Alastair flicked the metal lasso so that it sparked against the pavement, lighting up the dark night. He raised his arm, letting it fly through the air, uncoiling to snap near her ribcage, but the bird never flinched. Wu opened her shoulders, her wingspan stretching over the fire escape. She lifted off, hovering over him like a dark cloud. Her black silhouette blotted out the stars. Alastair twirled the whip higher. She landed on another fire escape and laughed, which sounded like a keening cry. Alastair reeled in his lasso, patiently waiting her out. "Come on, you tough old bird, show me what you've got!" he called, standing defiantly in the open, daring her to attack.

Wu screeched in outrage, turning her beady gaze on him. She leaned forward, launching herself in a dive aimed directly at his chest. Alastair waited, his fingers squeezing the coils of his lasso so hard his knuckles turned white. "Come on," he said quietly. He felt the air currents change and smelled the fetid odor of death. With a flick of his wrist, he threw the heavy chain directly at the plummeting bird, expertly pinning the wings against Wu's heaving sides. Wu pulled herself away, propelling herself against a wall, stretching the whip to its fullest extent. Alastair struggled, planting his feet, using the dumpster for leverage. He pressed a lever that set mechanical gears in motion, reeling in the long chain. Wu strained against the chain, but Alastair held on, his knuckles white. He felt his body shake with the strain, but he closed his mind to everything but pulling in the bird.

"Alastair!" Wes yelled.

"It's as easy as flying a kite," he called back, fighting to keep control of the hawk. "Get. Her. Out of here!" He smiled. "What goes up … must come …" He yanked the chain, watching it squeeze the breath from Wu, who plummeted, landing in a heap of leather and feathers at his feet, "down." She immediately morphed into herself. "Hello, ol' thing." He reached into his pocket, took out the roll of duct tape, and quickly placed a generous amount across her mouth, sealing it from uttering a spell. Resting his booted foot on the winded woman, he asked, "Now, what's so special about the shipment?"

Wu's garbled response did not appear to be helpful. Narrowing her eyes, she kicked out, missing him.

"Hm. Where in the world are we going to put you?" Alastair said, bending down so that his breath fell on her face.

Wu snarled, her arms fighting against the chain. A cell phone broke the silence.

"I believe it's for you, but being you're tied up at the moment—pun intended—allow me." Alastair plucked the phone from her breast pocket. Blowing gently, he dislodged a dark feather.

He swiped the screen to answer and put the phone to his ear.

"Wu?" a voice demanded. "Do you have her? Wu?"

"Bernadette," Alastair said flatly.

"Alastair." The line went dead.

CHAPTER FIFTEEN

M y sister keeps a change of clothes here in case of snow."
Wes opened the closet, taking out a pair of jogging
pants and a shirt.

"Why?" called Morgan from the bathroom, where she had
finished a shower.

"She works in the city but lives on the island. Sometimes
she stays here if the weather's bad and she can't go home." Wes
held up the pants, sizing them.

"Too long," Morgan said from the hallway, towel drying her
hair.

"We can cut them down."

"I don't want to do that," Morgan said. "They're not mine."

"I'll replace them. Trust me, she won't mind."

Morgan walked toward the window, sniffing. "Smells good.
Greek?" she asked, pointing down. "I'm hungry. I'm not going
to let you ruin her clothes."

"Oh, enough already." Junie walked in from the kitchen.
She grabbed the pants, swung them in a circle, snapped them
once, then handed the perfectly shortened pants back to Wes.

He stared at them, incredulous. When Alastair had decided to put Junie in a safe house, it turned out to be Wes's apartment.

"How'd you get in here?" Wes asked.

"Alastair sent me to chaperone. He said your joint was as good as any for me to lay low. Hey, I did your laundry."

"I don't have a washer." Wes looked around at his tidied apartment.

"I don't need no machines." Junie winked. Luna meowed loudly and Junie looked down. "Yes, I forgot. I've got something in the oven."

"I don't have an oven," Wes said.

"Apparently you do now. Who's that?" Morgan asked, taking the pants.

"Hi, doll." Junie held out her hand. "Junie 'Bags' Meadows. I knew your mother. I made dinner." She returned to the tiny kitchen. "Nice place you got here for being out in the country."

"It's Queens." Wes followed her to see what she was concocting. "Where'd you get that?" he asked, seeing a tray filled with sandwiches.

"Look, kid, if you're not going to like the answers, don't ask the questions." She pointed to a book on the counter called *Seven Tricks for the Dyslexic*. "You know, I can fix that, if you want."

Wes ignored her.

He returned to the living room to see Morgan sitting on the couch brushing her hair on the couch. "I hope you don't mind. It's all tangled."

"Be my guest." He watched the muted light of the room play with the hidden depths of color in her hair. He'd thought it was black but had never realized the many different layers of darkness that could be identified. Violet vied with a rich blue in her thick mane. She brushed vigorously, and her hair crackled with static, sparks flying with each movement of her hand. He moved closer, closing his strong fingers around hers. Their eyes met and time seemed to stop.

Morgan shook her hand loose. "You're not my type."

"What's your type?"

She stood up and moved away, nervous about the attraction she felt. "Not you." She turned her attention to the kitchen, calling out, "What do you mean, you knew my mother?"

Wes watched her leave, wondering why the room felt so empty when she left it.

Junie was busy chopping fruit when Morgan entered the kitchen. She looked up, acknowledging the young girl. "Took you long enough."

"My mother?"

"Catarina. The prettier of the two sisters."

"You know Bea?"

"Like the back of my hand." She held up the wrinkled hand.

"They were identical, I was told."

"Only on the outside," Junie said cryptically. "I used to babysit for them before they moved to Manhattan. I knew the whole family."

"Did you know my father?"

Wes joined them, and Junie shrugged.

"Well, did you?"

Junie looked as Alastair entered the room.

"Wu?" Wes asked.

"Animal control has her. I'm kidding. She's in a special holding cell at Central. Did you look at the USB?"

Wes shook his head guiltily.

"Well, go get it," Alastair ordered.

"Is Gabby all right?" Morgan asked, forgetting about Junie.

"Sleeping safe and sound, all creepy critters back in candy form. You know she won't remember anything."

"I didn't mean for her to be in danger. I don't understand what's going on. Bea has changed."

Alastair shook his head. "She hasn't changed—you're just seeing her for the first time."

"What are you talking about?" she demanded. "You don't know us. She raised me! She's been like a mother to me since I was two."

"Was she really like a mother?" Alastair asked.

"Bernadette is hard and ambitious. She expects the same from everyone around her. This whole face cream thing is crazy. It's like she is being driven by something strange."

"There's nothing on it." Wes dashed into the room, holding up the small plastic USB.

"Impossible. Let me see."

He brought in his laptop. "Look, it's blank." He pushed it in the port as they breathlessly watched the empty screen. "It's been erased."

"The formula. All the shipment information was on there. It was all for nothing!"

"What's so special about this cream?" Wes asked.

Morgan paused.

"Really, Morgan. Who are you protecting and why?" Wes yelled. "You could have been killed tonight."

"Not unless I was a diabetic," Morgan replied.

"Ha, ha, funny. What do you think that birdbrain had in mind for you?"

"He has a point, sweetie," Junie told her. "Maybe you think you're protecting your aunt by doing this. I can tell you something, nothing good is going on."

Morgan bit her lip, looking at each of them, from Junie's rubbery visage to Alastair's pinched, pale face.

She sighed loudly. "Any woman applying Glow will have the Bernadette Pendragon's DNA seeping into her skin.

Bernadette will be linked to them and plans to exert influence. She is looking toward world domination."

"That's crazy!" Wes said.

"See what I mean? He doesn't understand." Morgan smirked.

"Explain it so he can," Alastair said gently.

"It's not crazy. The women apply the cream. Then, when they see an ad or hear one on the radio, something clicks, and voilà—they will buy up any product my aunt has an interest in. She's been purchasing small companies all over the country for some time."

"Like what? Wes asked.

"She bought Genie Wilson's weight-loss meals, Comstock Department Stores. I know she's in negotiation with Dexter Computers, and last week she purchased a television network."

"So, the whole thing is about money," Wes said flatly. "Big deal. Magazines and television have been influencing buyers for years. An actress or celebrity only has to wear something or use a product, and every consumer is out buying it off the shelves. I don't think that's so important. She just stands to get that much richer." Wes thought for a minute. "Anyway, if she bought a station, it would have made all the papers."

"Not if you purchase with a partner nobody knows about," Alastair said thoughtfully.

Morgan's jaw dropped. "She's been meeting with—"

"Vice President Gilroy's wife, Juliet Gilroy," Junie said grimly.

"How did you know?" Morgan turned to stare at the older woman.

"I saw an image. I wasn't sure if it was her. In my stew," Junie said.

"Why didn't you say something?" Alastair asked.

"It was hazy. Besides, she's always been Davina."

"The vice president's wife?" Wes asked.

"She's going to be the next president of the United States," Morgan said with astonishment.

"What makes you say that?"

"Something Bea said." Morgan looked thoughtful. "She told her to behave like the leader she was supposed to be."

"I highly doubt that. She can't sell her cream to every female, and even if she influences millions of women, that's still only half the vote," Wes argued.

"Not so much, pretty boy," Junie said. "Which way the neck turns, so does the head. She plans on reaching women who will in turn influence their men."

"I can't believe witches are so close to the White House," Wes said.

"Honey, there are witches *in* the White House. How else do you think those morons get elected?" Junie laughed.

"That's nuts!"

"Davinas have been key players for years. It was our job to keep the Willas at bay."

"So what's gone wrong?"

"My aunt turned," Morgan said. "That's what's wrong, and she's gotten so powerful they may not be able to contain her. It's crazy; she wants to rule the world."

"Holy crap," Wes muttered.

"More like unholy, I think," Alastair added grimly.

"Why hasn't anyone stopped her? You know, like the FDA?"

"She's been lying about the contents. Besides, who knows who is on her payroll there?" Morgan said.

"Those shipments are hitting the high seas in a little over twenty-four hours. We've got to stop her," Junie said fiercely.

"What about the distribution in this country?" Wes asked.

"That's still under our control. Once those creams are

dropped off in foreign ports, we won't be able to stop her," Alastair told him. "You can't accuse her without proof."

"Jersey. We have to get to the plant in Fort Lee, New Jersey," Morgan said. "I can get into the warehouse there. We can reload the USB with the information and take it to the right authorities."

Wes turned to Alastair. "You're not thinking of bringing Junie and Morgan, are you?"

"Do you have a better plan? Morgan knows exactly what she's looking for."

Morgan looked at Wes, her eyes intense. "You're not going without me. I have to stop her before she goes too far."

"Don't you think she has already?"

"Look, Wes. Willas turn up every now and then and make trouble. It's always been avoidable. People like Alastair have been steps ahead of them."

"Not this time," Wes told her.

"True," Junie continued. "Truth is, it's never gone this far before. No Willa has ever been able to get this powerful."

"So what happened?"

"I don't know. I just don't know," Alastair said, but Junie knew that was not the truth.

Wes sighed. "I'll get the car."

Luna meowed loudly and Junie laughed. "I know. Road trip!"

CHAPTER SIXTEEN

G et the ads up and running!" Bernadette ordered. "I want my face cream in every store by the end of this week!"

Scarlett stood with a pad, writing instructions. The conference table was filled with personnel, each taking notes, waiting for Bernadette to reveal her plans.

Bernadette watched the reaction of her dream team, the *crème de la crème* of fashion, beauty products, magazines, and finance gathered at her quartz table. The room buzzed with energy. She had looted the most prolific and successful companies across the globe, recruiting the smartest and most aggressive women in business. This was her own personal shark tank. If they couldn't find anything to eat, they'd feed on each other, and most weren't even witches! Lila Duran, head of publicity, stood in her pinstripe Prada suit. She pulled at her straight hair nervously.

"I haven't done a press release, other than that rather half-assed taradiddle about the bird and panther. Really, Bern, I need a few more days." She had a British accent that revealed a history attending the private schools of the very privileged.

"Well, Lil," Bernadette said from the head of the table. "You don't have it." She walked before a tripod holding an eraser board with a timeline on it. She passed the smallest rock in her hands from palm to palm. "Maybe if you spent less time in DJ Wub It Out's bed, you'd have more time to get the work done."

"That's just a rumor." Lila's skin pinkened. "We attended Kanye's show in Paris and sat next to each other."

"Tell that to his wife. You're lucky I like you." Bernadette sniffed. "Look, I'm not one to pass judgment, but when work has to get done, get it done."

"I have to coordinate with the studios. We have a movie featuring the cream in the story line. You can't spring this on me at the last minute."

"Really," Bernadette replied sarcastically. "What a whole lot of work you'll have to do tonight, then. Right, Lil?" She drew out the name ominously.

"Is there even enough product on hand for the stores?" Roni Ellen, head of sales, asked. Her glasses slipped down her wide nose, burned brown from a tanning booth she had in her office, one of the perks of being head of sales. There was very little Bernadette denied her staff. "I've promised two hundred million units, but if there is a run on Glow, this could be a disaster. People will mob the stores ..." Her voice started rising with panic. "The suppliers might get angry. We could lose credibility! Where's Wu? I need her to contact our factories in Singapore."

"Wu's out of town," Bernadette said dismissively.

"But I need her," Roni implored, her voice dying as she took in Bernadette's cold stare.

"Well, you'll have to manage without her." She smiled coldly at the women. "Ladies, ladies, please." Bernadette held her hands up, revealing that each palm now cradled one of her round stones. The room calmed. "I don't pay you these exorbitant salaries to go out to lunch and hobnob with the *hoi polloi* on my dime for nothing. Lila, you were nothing but a blow-up doll for your former boss. Yeah, sure, he let you use the company plane, but what did that do for you? Charlotte"—she turned to the sleek woman who was head of legal— "you covered your old boss's Ponzi scheme, then bailed him out after the cops came, right, counselor? Roni"—she pointed to her suntanned face— "was hiding her former employer's expenses from the government—a jailable offense last time I looked— and Sybil, I don't want to even get into the gunrunning with the hotel asshole you worked for. Last time I looked I had a group of women who were able to accomplish everything possible legally as well as illegally. All I asked for was to move up a distribution time." Bernadette's voice ricocheted off the black walls. The room was deathly silent. She placed the rocks on the table before her. Everybody knew about the rocks. Bernadette had a reputation for fondling them. Most thought it was unnerving. No one knew of their crystal strength, able to open Bernadette's cluttered mind, zeroing in on her need to focus, dissolving the chaos. Scarlett thought they had powers. Bernadette never explained their abilities were wholly personal. Only Morgan intuitively felt them.

The door burst open. A stocky woman in a tight blue business suit, her fat, dimpled legs unattractively stuffed into low-heeled leather shoes, rushed into the room. Her short, frosted hair was combed ruthlessly to the side, and her faded blue eyes were wild with fear. "Bernadette!" she shouted.

Jasmine clutched the doorknob, still trying to prevent the intrusion. Her pitiful, acne-encrusted face turned nervously toward her boss. "I tried to keep her out," she explained, her voice small.

Bernadette pasted a welcoming smile on her taut face. She turned to her staff. "Any questions?"

The room filled with a chorus of, "No problem!" "On it,

boss" and "You'll have it on your desk within the hour." They filed out of the room, their worried, ashen faces distracted by the overnighter they were about to pull.

"Never mind, Jasmine." Bernadette waved her off as the room emptied. "Scarlett, do something about her face. I can't look at it anymore. Besides, it's bad for business. We *are* in skincare." She motioned for them to leave. "Juliet, what brings you to New York?" she asked brightly.

Scarlett rolled her eyes with halfhearted agreement. "All right, come on," she told the pock-faced assistant.

"They know something!" Juliet paced the room. "They are on to us. Bernadette, Larry has been asking too many questions."

"It's all under control, Juliet. You know that. We've planned for years. Sit down." She gestured at the seat before her desk. Bernadette sat down in her big leather chair, resting her thin arms on the stone top. She wanted to remind Juliet who was boss. "What kind of questions?"

"They took Larry in yesterday. He didn't say much, but they wanted to know about Bonsai Investments." Bonsai was the company they'd used to buy the network. "What could he say? He doesn't know anything about it." Juliet worried her lip.

"Just as he shouldn't," Bernadette assured her.

"They asked if … if I still practiced, and would he vouch that I'm … Davina." Juliet rose. "I knew I should have stayed with the old ways." She got up, pacing the room.

Bernadette walked around, placing a comforting arm around her shoulders. "Too late for that now, my dear. Who questioned you?"

"I don't know. I don't know who they are. FBI, police, I don't know if they even told me," she added with horrified wonder. "They were armed, with Trance Lifters. I thought you couldn't even get those anymore. This is terrible. We have to close it down."

"Knockoffs, I'm sure. They don't make them; they're obsolete. Come now, Juliet. The invitations are out."

"What invitations?" Juliet asked, her eyes popping out of her head.

"Figuratively speaking, the invitations to your inaugural ball, Madam President. Stop worrying. I have it all under control."

"You promised no one would put it together. You swore, Bernadette."

"I never break my word. Your reputation will be safe. No one will know. We shall announce your candidacy just as we planned. Let me handle everything. Ah, Scarlett, you're back. Please escort Mrs. Gilroy back to her car." She turned to Juliet. "Juliet, remember what I told you. We can't be seen together just yet." She wagged a finger at her. "Don't come here again."

Scarlett escorted Juliet out. Bernadette spun her chair to look outside. In the window, cat's eyes reflected back at her. She turned back to her open office door. "Where are they, Vincenza?"

Vincenza held a large bowl filled with clear liquid in her hands. She blew on the surface gently, watching the water ripple from a tiny circle growing larger until it filled the entire bowl.

"Vincenza!" Bernadette said sharply.

"Patience. I see the car." A black SUV materialized on the surface of the water. Four faces appeared.

"Is she there?" Bernadette demanded.

Vincenza nodded without looking up. "Yes, with an old man, the young one I bit, and ..."

"And?"

"One of us."

Vincenza dipped her finger in the bowl, circling the image

of the older woman. "One of us, yet not one of us. They go to Jersey."

"Jersey?"

"The warehouse," Vincenza confirmed.

"Stop them. Bring my niece to me."

Vincenza looked at her. "I may have to use my magic out in the open. We don't have much time."

Bernadette frowned. "It doesn't matter anymore."

Vincenza placed the bowl on Bernadette's desk, closing the door quietly behind her. Bernadette looked at the quaking water but saw nothing.

Scarlett stood in the outer office, looking up when Vincenza entered the room.

Vincenza smiled slyly. "You know what I want," she told Scarlett, her eyes leering at her lush body.

"You get me what I want," Scarlett said in a sultry whisper, "and I'll give you what you want."

Vincenza gave a ferocious growl, her eyes blazing as she bounded toward the elevator.

CHAPTER SEVENTEEN

An hour later, the four found themselves in bumper-to-bumper traffic on the George Washington Bridge. Morgan and Junie sat in the rear. Alastair drove, which left Wes riding shotgun.

"I told you we should have taken the tunnel," Wes said sourly.

"You saw the news. It was backed up for miles. Besides, Fort Lee is right over the bridge," Alastair shot back.

Alastair's rifle lay comfortably against Wes's leg, the heavy weight of it reassuring him. Still hazy on the details, Wes remained skeptical about the whole thing. He couldn't wrap his head around the idea of witches. Every so often, he caught a glimpse of Morgan, her worried face in shadow. *She couldn't be a witch,* he thought. She didn't look like one. He glanced over at Junie and shuddered.

Twice, Morgan quietly asked the older woman about her mother, and the conversation was deftly turned away. Junie seemed reluctant to share details, which irritated Morgan. She stared out the window sullenly.

"I don't like it, Alastair," Junie grumbled. Luna arched her back, hissing. "Where?" Junie demanded, but the cat didn't answer.

"Look," Morgan said quietly.

A giant billboard was illuminated in the night sky. On it, one of the most iconic women in the music industry looked out, her face glowing. "Pendragon Glow for those in the know" read the advertisement. "Available in stores worldwide Monday. Perfect for Mother's Day!"

"It's starting," Morgan said. "She planned a July release, but she's doing it earlier."

"She senses something," Alastair said quietly.

"Never mind that old bat. I sense something, too!" Junie leaned forward, her face between the two seats. She pointed to a commotion in front of them. "I think the world is going to rediscover witches real soon."

Wes bent down to peer through the windshield.

He heard Alastair curse as he slowed to a dead stop and unbuckled his seat belt. "Get out," he ordered.

"We're on a bridge. Where do you want me to go?"

"It's Vincenza," Morgan stated upon seeing the dark-haired beauty circling the bridge, a broom between her leather-clad legs.

Wes chuckled. "You've got to be kidding me."

"Looks like witches have come out of the closet," Junie said.

"Yeah," Wes retorted. "The broom closet."

The bridge was a sea of red lights, horns honking. People exited their autos, holding up cell phones to record. Some were laughing. Others shouted, pointing to Vincenza, who sneered back. The moon bathed her in an eerie glow, and the sky was strangely vacant of stars.

Alastair walked briskly to the back of the SUV, opening the

hatch to reveal a veritable arsenal of Steampunk weapons. The others followed him.

He grabbed a handful of flares, spreading them out in front of them. He lit one. The beacon painted his face red. Wes looked up and shivered, thinking he resembled something demonic.

Junie rubbed her hands together gleefully. "Flares! Oh, how I love flares!"

"She looks pissed off." Morgan watched the circling sorceress, her pattern moving around them lazily.

"You think?" Wes asked sarcastically.

"In a minute, the cops are going to get here. They will have every driver exit their cars and walk back to Manhattan. Get Morgan out of here." Alastair turned back to the truck, opening and rummaging around a huge red toolbox. Wes thought he looked worried—not necessarily a good sign.

"I'm not leaving you," Wes declared.

"You don't have to worry about us. Oh, Alastair, an Aether Cannon." Junie sounded pleased. "I always wanted to hold one of those."

Alastair was busy loading the toast-colored weapon, the Tesla coils lighting up with a blue phosphorus glow, the gears making a whining sound that reminded Wes of a dental drill.

"What's your Gamertag?" Wes asked with a laugh.

"I-AM-WHAT-I-AM, all dashes in between," Alastair retorted.

"Mine's Johnny Depth. One word."

"Original." Alastair smiled.

"I thought so," Wes replied, enjoying the moment.

"Really? Can we cool it with the Kumbaya moment?" Morgan screamed.

Vincenza swooped down, her broom creating a hot breeze as she flew past them. Some people screamed, others were laughing and pointing, and several started a stampede off the bridge. The sound of multiple sirens grew louder.

Wes calmly looked at the woman who was watching them with menacing intensity. "What kind of witch is that?"

"Level four Willa," Alastair responded. "Sort of a soldier, trained in Europe—Italy, to be exact."

"The panther?" Wes asked, his foot beginning to throb.

"She likes snakes, too," Morgan volunteered.

Junie whistled. "That's a problem." There was no time to explain. The bridge was swarming with police. Vincenza landed on a cable and hung on like a diabolical pirate in a storm. Laying her broom sideways, she swung in a circle, wrapping her legs around the thick cables. Catcalls and whistles along with raucous shouts drifted up to her. She obliged, draping herself upside down and doing an impromptu interpretation of a pole dance.

Wes and Alastair paused, watching with the same appreciation of nineteen-year-old boys in a strip club.

"She's got talent," Alastair murmured.

"Yeah, real talent," Morgan retorted. "You should see what she does with a feather and—"

An officer holding a megaphone called out to Vincenza, interrupting Morgan. "Ma'am, get down from there!" Black-clad SWAT officers crept through the congested lanes.

Vincenza laughed, the sound bouncing off the choppy waves below them.

"Uh-oh, here it comes," Junie warned.

Vincenza lifted her arm as she spoke. "Take these suspension cables and make them break, give the bridge and tunnel people a slithery, slimy snake. One snake, two snakes, three snakes, four. Make them all too big to ignore!"

The air stilled. The restive crowd became silent. Thunder boomed and the air turned static. Wes could feel his hair rise from the top of his scalp. The atmosphere felt thick with antici-pation; sounds were muted, as if they were wrapped in cotton batting.

Four of the twenty khaki-colored suspension cables writhed with a loud creaking sound, startling the onlookers. The coils stretched, then recoiled, finally detaching with a hissing sound and rocking the bridge, as if it were in an earthquake. The thick cables moved sensuously, their surfaces transforming to a shiny, spotted green. The cables rose, dangling over the cars, now with giant, shovel-like heads, forked tongues dancing from their sinister faces. People screamed with fear, some racing, leaving cars abandoned. Others stood in frozen horror, watching in mute shock as the snakes made their way to the canted surface of the bridge. Four sets of beady, bright-yellow eyes scanned the screaming crowd. They slithered down. The bridge groaned, leaning to one side. Cars smashed into one another, setting off multiple alarms. Luna screeched, jumping onto the roof of the truck, then took off, leaping from car to car across the bridge toward Jersey.

"What are you going to do?" Wes yelled over the din.

Alastair shoved a bystander out of the way, positioning the cannon on the rear of the person's car. "I told you to get out of here before it's too late."

Another driver hung down from the door of his semi. He eyed the strange weaponry in front of Alastair. "You ain't gonna do nuthin' with that lil' toy gun." He reached into his cab, taking out a twelve-gauge.

The snakes moved closer, their spitting and hissing drowning out the cries of the mob scene below. One reptile was on the blacktop, ducking under cars in its attempt to reach the SUV. Junie ran forward, stopping in a wide stance to aim her gun. A gelatinous globe exploded from the muzzle. The recoil rocked her arms so that they shook with strain. She fired off four shots, driving the crowd into a frenzy of fear. "You have to get them between the eyes," she called out. One snake's head evaporated in a shower of blood and bone. The crowd was incoherent.

"Nice shooting!" the truck driver yelled. Turning, he laughed good-naturedly blasting away at the second snake threatening them from the cables to the left.

"Follow Luna," Junie advised Wes. "Here she goes again."

More shots were fired. Vincenza ignored them, cackling with malice. She observed the fleeing people who were fighting the stream of SWAT members forcing their way toward her. Glancing to where the blond man held Morgan's hand with the older, white-haired man, she eyed the cars on the bridge, looking for something to slow them up. She spied an abandoned oil tanker on the other side of the divider.

"Toil, toil, bubble, and boil. Give me a stream of dark, slick oil." The tanker burst open as if a bomb had exploded, its deluge of black oil pushing back the advancing police. She made eye contact with Alastair and pointed to him. Then, her two fingers gestured at her eyes as if to acknowledge she was watching him.

Alastair saw her motioning to him but avoided her gaze. He watched the pandemonium, muttering, "Well, that's already on Twitter."

Junie aimed her pistol at the enemy, firing blasts of the goopy pellets that fell short only to splatter on cars, dripping down like melting cake icing. Vincenza grabbed her broom and straddled it, ignoring the crowd. Alastair saw her eyes were on Morgan. He crouched down, taking aim.

"Look, if I miss my shot, she's going to grab Morgan. I mean it, get out of here."

Wes pulled Morgan's hand and began sprinting through the crowd toward the far side of the bridge.

Two helicopters, one on each side of the bridge, moved closer, the rotors buffeting against the wind. A sharpshooter leaned out, pointing a rifle at the witch. Wes could feel the vibration of the blades, the sound drowned by the booming thunder shaking the sky. Lightning scored the horizon, turning the sea into a churning mess. The loudspeaker broke through the noise again, asking the woman to turn herself in.

Vincenza sneered and flew a loop around them, causing the helicopters to follow her. She spiraled downward then pulled up, veering away after a near-collision of the two choppers. Below them in the water, police boats aimed high-powered beams upward, bathing the air show in bright light. Rain started to fall, dazzling the lights and painting everything silver. Vincenza moved in an upward arc; one chopper followed, then stalled. It hovered for an instant before plummeting into the water, landing with a crash like a smashed mosquito.

Alastair watched Vincenza spin to attack the remaining chopper. He closed one eye, making sure the witch was in his crosshairs. She bounced, righting herself while holding the broomstick with two hands. Alastair pressed the lever, letting go a blast of white foam. It reached the straw of her broom, igniting it so that it flared in the dark sky. Vincenza reached behind, batting it with her palm, the helicopter forgotten.

Some of the fluid dripped onto the asphalt, sizzling like acid. Junie touched it with the tip of her finger, then grimaced when it burned her fingertip. "What is that stuff?" She wiped her burnt finger on her skirt.

Alastair didn't answer. Vincenza had turned, her face white with rage. She threw back her head, calling to the heavens to give them more, and the sky roiled with heavy, dark clouds. Thunder boomed and lightning flashed, splitting the black night. The heavens opened and torrents of rain flooded the bridge. She turned, aiming the point of her broomstick downward, a trail of white smoke following from her damaged broom. She screamed, directing the storm to flood the bridge.

Alastair ignored the splashing rain running down his face. He shot directly at her, but she weaved between the missiles which flew harmlessly past her, falling into the water with a hiss.

Alastair cursed loudly. The cannon jammed, overheating and dripping white fluid on the back of the car, burning the paint off. Everything sizzled and bubbled. A haze of smoke rose from the steaming pavement. He looked up to see Vincenza heading right for him. Something tugged at his foot.

Junie called out, "Look out, Alastair!" Her face frozen with fear, her eyes were glued to the snake that had him by the ankle. She struggled with two policemen, her arms imprisoned. The officer snatched her gun.

A snake inched up Alastair's leg underneath is trouser. It hissed against his calf. The reptile's cold tongue flickered on his skin, sending goose bumps down his spine. He could feel the snake squeeze gently, building pressure until his leg went numb. Police were now shooting, their bullets useless against the Willa. Vincenza screamed as she descended, her eyes dark pits of hell, her mouth pulled back in a grimace of hatred. She was heading directly for Alastair.

Rain slashed against them, creating great pools of black water. The bridge swayed dangerously.

Morgan slipped on oil, bringing both her and Wes down in a tangle. Wes pulled her up, their clothes clinging to their slick bodies. He heard Vincenza's earsplitting howl and realized she was on a collision course for Alastair, who seemed frozen. He opened a car door, shoved Morgan in, then climbed onto the car's top, leaping onto a Mack truck's cab. Gasping for air, he dashed a hand in front of his wet eyes, brushing away the driving rain.

Standing with his feet planted on the slippery roof of the cab, he aimed the awkward handgun at the witch's back, waiting for the perfect shot. Swallowing hard, he pressed the trigger with steady hands, not really sure what to expect. Small pulses reverberated up his arms, causing them to shake. He looked incredulously for bullets, seeing nothing but a disturbance in the air. The rain appeared to waver, but he saw no discharge. A delayed blast shook the listing bridge. The powerful burst of energy hit the witch squarely in the back. She fell forward, losing speed and careening into a red van. Stunned, her leg took the brunt of the impact, her knuckles holding the stick of her broom tightly. She growled, kicking out and lifting off again.

"What kind of gun is this?" he shouted.

"It's sort of a cosmic super soaker. Hit the bitch again!" Morgan yelled. She was standing on the roof of the next car. She jumped across, slipping. Wes grabbed her under the arm so that they stood close together.

"Get inside!" he screamed at her.

Morgan was ready to argue but saw Vincenza had turned and was heading toward them at an astonishing speed.

The witch snarled as she gathered momentum, racing toward Wes. Wes pushed Morgan behind him. Engaging in his firing stance, he held his arms out, waiting for the perfect shot. Vincenza cackled with ugly glee, speed making her twisted smile stretch as if she were looking in a funhouse mirror. The rain plastered his shirt against his body. His feet began to slide on the wet surface of the vehicle.

"Don't look at her eyes," Morgan advised him.

Wes nodded, holding his breath; the world narrowed to the two of them. The air changed as she sped toward him. He fired, watching the impact throw her backward. She somersaulted, her broom flying out from underneath her and cracking in half. She bounced on the stretched cable, flying high, then tipped into the ocean. Vincenza screamed as she hit the water. Wes watched as the sea foamed, turning a rainbow of colors, the surface churning, pulling the disintegrating witch into its cold depths. The rain eased, then stopped completely. The silence swelled as the remaining cables yawed.

The snake gripping Alastair uncoiled and fell harmlessly onto the pavement, turning into a mass of unraveled wires.

Wes jumped down and turned to lift Morgan. Holding hands, they ran back to Alastair and Junie.

"Nice work. Head to Fort Lee."

"You're not coming?"

Alastair shook his head. "I've got some explaining to do. Someone has to stay and clean this up. Leave before they pull you in for questioning." He turned to walk over to a squad car, a sincere smile on his face.

"What kind of badge is this?" demanded the officer who identified himself as Captain Halperin. He was as white-haired as Alastair, with the thickened middle of constant desk work. His nose told of his taste for a good drink after work. Alastair handed him his flask.

"Can't. On the job." Halperin shrugged. "I've never seen this badge before." He squinted at Alastair's shield.

Alastair took his arm. "I suggest you call this number." He handed him a card with the seal of the Commissioner on it.

"You stay right here." He directed two men to keep watch on Alastair and Junie.

Halperin disappeared into an unmarked car and emerged twenty minutes later, his face white with shock. "You still got that little flask?" he asked Alastair.

Alastair was leaning against the opened door of a pickup truck. Junie had a crowd of officers around her, laughing at something she was relating about the Red Hook Port.

Alastair reached into his chest pocket and handed him the flask with a companionable smile.

"Hard to believe," the officer said after a long pull.

"Once you really get to know them, it's hard to believe you didn't see it sooner." Alastair paused. "So did we make the papers?"

Halperin laughed. "The papers, Twitter, YouTube, Instagram. Witches are trending, my friend, and you are being called the Witch Hunter."

"The Witch Hunter? That could hardly be further from the truth."

"Won't be long before Hollywood calls," Halperin said, handing back the flask. "You, my friend, are the man of the hour."

CHAPTER EIGHTEEN

W es called an Uber to meet him on the other side of the bridge. Sliding into the quiet confines of the car, he shook his head to the inquiries of the driver.

"What happened back there?" the driver asked insistently.

"A cable broke."

"A cable?"

"Yeah, snapped and uncoiled like a snake." Wes gave the address, then fell backward next to Morgan, not even realizing they were still holding hands. Disengagement was awkward. Wes mumbled an apology, to which Morgan responded just as uncomfortably. They pulled into a deserted industrial park, asking the driver to let them out around the corner from the Pendragon building.

The wind had died down. The sky cleared, revealing a sparkling canvas of stars. Wes searched upward, his eyes finding the constellation Hydra. Morgan gazed up, asking, "What are you looking for?"

He pointed to a long chain of stars. "That's Hydra. Hercules slew Hydra. It had multiple heads that kept growing back."

"One of Hercules's twelve labors," she whispered back, showing she knew Greek mythology, too. "Pendragon is like the hydra. There are many heads that are going to grow back."

Wes shrugged, feeling like he had aged a lifetime. Beliefs had been ripped apart. His whole world had changed. Nothing would ever be the same again.

"Are you a witch, too?"

Morgan shivered, wondering exactly how to answer him. "Sometimes. Does that bother you?" she asked, afraid of his answer.

Wes looked at her face, her dark eyes, the sweep of her lashes. "Everybody has something."

"Do you?"

Wes looked at the logo on the sign that indicated they were at Pendragon's warehouses. He slowly unscrambled the letters, sighing. "Let's go get this hydra." They skirted the walkway, using a grassy lawn and diving between clumps of bushes.

A guard rounded the corner. The two intruders stood in the lee of a garden, knee-deep in the bushes. "They'll never let us pass."

"Let me think."

"Don't you have a plan?" Morgan whispered furiously.

"We have to get inside this complex. I'll come up with something."

Morgan hesitated, then said tentatively, "I can put a spell on us."

"Yeah, you can turn us into frogs," Wes said dismissively. "Let me think."

Morgan cocked her head, biting her bottom lip. "Then we can hop our way in."

"I was kidding," Wes whispered back frantically. "You're not going to turn us into … What are you doing?" He bent down where she was gathering a small pile of twigs and dirt. "Stop that!" He brushed her hands away.

"Shush," she calmly replied, back in her element. "It's a great idea. It's not like you're going to stay a frog."

"I'm not doing this."

Morgan reached over to tear a small twig off a thin tree branch. It broke after she twisted hard. She pointed the jagged branch at the doorway, gauging the distance to the entrance. "We'll have, like, six minutes to hop from here to the main entrance."

"Are you crazy?"

Morgan looked up at his worried face and placed a grubby hand on his cheek. Her eyes softened, and she wet her lips. Wes's world narrowed, relegating frogs, witches, and face cream to the furthest corner of his mind.

He leaned down, his lips tentatively meeting hers. Their mouths molded together. His arms surrounded her, pulling her close. When her tongue touched his, he groaned, deepening the kiss.

Morgan pulled away, a smile teasing her lips. "The kiss comes after, silly. Now, when I say inhale, breathe deep. Hop, hop, hop is the easiest of the codes to turn us into a couple of toads. Now breathe!" Holding the branch over their heads, Morgan blew a pile of dried leaves from her palm into his face.

Wes choked on the dust, his eyes bulging out of his head. His skin became tight. A cold chill traveled up his spine. The world receded; sound stretched in his ears. He felt dizzy. His chest constricted, then expanded, air rushing through him. Lights grew fuzzy, then elongated, filling his line of vision with striated neon streaks. He opened his mouth to complain, and a loud croak came out. He looked up, realizing he was staring at a large rock that was formerly a mere pebble. Morgan batted her froggy eyes at him, her tiny green derriere wiggling as she led the way. Wes cursed, hearing Morgan giggle at his complaining ribbiting. He looked down at his splayed amphibious hands. A faint buzzing filled his ears. *Do frogs even have ears?* he wondered. He spied a firefly lazily dipping behind drooping blossoms. Tilting his head, he felt a faint urge to roll out his long tongue to catch the bug. He heard Morgan impatiently whisper, "Come on. We can catch a bite later." So he did what any frog would do—he hopped after her.

The path was a tangled mess, filled with dew-laden ferns that slashed against his face as he followed Morgan. His protruding eyes rolled in his head. He looked up at the distant stars, cursing hydras, witches, and the new reality he found himself in. Wes called out for Morgan to slow down. It came out in a loud croak, but she seemed to understand him, turning around to bat those dark, long-lashed wet eyes. Wes moaned as his gullet swelled, and a cacophony of sounds erupted. Morgan listened intently, then responded with an equal amount of ribbiting that seemed to make weird sense. *Head for the door. It's motion-activated, and we'll hop in. The guard won't be alarmed when he realizes it's just a couple of frogs,* she told him through her musical croaking.

Wes looked at the long distance between them and the awning of the entrance. He stared at the door, estimating the time needed to get there, when Morgan's gasp made him turn around. He felt his fear tighten his slimy skin when he saw a calico tabby crouching, ready to pounce.

"Run!" he croaked, turning to face the monster alone, his only thoughts for Morgan's safety. Inflating with air, he made himself a large target and watched those predatory eyes light on him, distracting the cat from Morgan. It was an alley cat, one ear torn, with the longest fangs he'd ever seen. Morgan inched behind him. He felt the cold wetness of her skin next to his. He kicked out with his long leg, pushing her as far away from him as he could. Their eyes made contact. He made a small sound, then leaped toward the feline. Morgan flew backward, a scream erupting from her mouth.

The cat meowed loudly as it pounced, its sharp claws scratching his delicate skin. He winced with pain, feeling his side tear just a bit. Inhaling, he jumped high, smacking the cat's face with his back flippers, hearing a satisfying crunch as he broke its front tooth. The cat yowled, spitting and hissing, using its paws to toy with him. Morgan hopped into the fray, hitting the cat's torso with her body, keeping up a sideways assault. The cat smacked back, sending Morgan into a sharp tangle of brambles. He heard the thud of her body as it was thrown into the thicket.

Wes yelled, "Morgan! Change us back!" There was no answering ribbit.

The cat used this distraction to grab Wes by the midsection with its bleeding mouth, shaking him as if he were a rag. The greenery whirled before his eyes in a nauseating kaleidoscope, and Wes knew with growing sadness he was doomed. He was going to die tonight, ending up the main course for Garfield. He wondered briefly if he'd taste like chicken.

A sharp incisor pierced the fragile flesh of his side. Wes thought of the serendipity of life. He liked Morgan, really liked her, and wished he had taken a moment to let her know. His father would never know what had happened to him and, for a second, Wes thought that would be the only good thing to come out of this debacle. Wes swelled, trying to drag air into his compressed lungs, but the cat held tight, the sound of traffic growing as faint as the distant stars in the sky. Though his vision dimmed, he looked longingly for Morgan, whom he now saw was splayed in a bush, her eyes closed.

He sighed with regret, croaking with surprise when his attacker screamed with anger. A black shadow flew past him, pouncing on the cat's back, causing his assailant to release him in a rush. He heard the high-pitched squeals of a catfight, hisses and spitting that ended with the calico escaping with a yowl into the night. Wes dragged air into his starved lungs, then felt the rough-edged caress of a cat's tongue on his skin. "Oh, not again." He sighed, turning to find the bright gaze of Luna watching him intently. She tapped him gently, pushing him toward Morgan, who smiled up at him groggily.

"Cat got your tongue?" Morgan croaked.

Wes could swear the cat snickered at him, but when he looked at her, he saw that Luna was looking pointedly toward a vent on the side of the building. Leading the way, Wes hopped toward the opening, Luna and Morgan following behind him. His side pained him, but adrenaline coursed through his small body. He felt a new determination replacing the lethargy that had enveloped him before.

The vent led to an internal office. Once Wes punched out the grill with his webbed feet, he leaped down, waiting for the others. Before she landed, Morgan managed to return them to their former state.

"What took you so long?" Wes asked breathlessly, pulling her into a tight embrace. She fit into the hollow of his arms, her head just under his chin. He ran urgent hands down her body, checking for injury.

Morgan giggled, her tentative fingers finding a tear in the skin on his flank. At Wes's quick intake of breath, she placed a comforting hand on the wound, which filled Wes's injured side with heat. She moved closer to him, brushing her lips against his, making them tingle with desire. "A kiss to make it better?" she whispered as if asking permission.

Wes gently took her head, feeling for a bump.

"Ow," Morgan complained.

"You deserve it for turning me into a frog."

"You technically still are without that kiss," Morgan whispered, standing on her tiptoes and wrapping her arms around his strong shoulders.

Wes leaned forward, his lips grazing hers as lightly as a summer breeze. Morgan felt her body start to hum with pleasure. She opened her mouth but was stopped abruptly by Luna's loud meow.

"What's she saying?" Wes asked, kissing her on the soft spot below her ear, sending waves of pleasure shivering through her body.

"She said to stop acting like cats in heat and get what we came here for."

Wes cleared his throat noisily. "So where do we go from here?" he asked.

Morgan took his hand, opened the door, and, after looking both ways down the hallway, headed to the lab.

Research and Development was tucked in the basement of the building, the room antiseptic and airtight. Rows of counters lined with Bunsen burners, assorted beakers, and long stretches of chalkboard covered with formulas filled the room. As he passed, Wes noticed different fragrances, some floral, some musky, but all attractive. Inside the lab was a glass door leading to an office. Morgan tried the knob, but it was locked. Wes spied a paperclip and swiped it from the countertop. He bent down and played with the lock. The tumblers clicked. They went in the room. Morgan sat in the chair behind the desk, typing the passwords to gain access to the computer. Wes opened a drawer of a filing cabinet, pulled out folders, and glanced through them.

"Wes," Morgan called, her face lit up by the screen. "I've got something."

He stood her, bending low to read the manifest. "Wow, that's a lot of face cream."

"It's the North American shipments. They haven't gone out yet."

"Can you cancel them?"

Morgan typed. The cat meowed loudly. "That's a good idea, Luna. She says to introduce a virus."

"Can you?"

Morgan shrugged. "I'll try."

Wes typed a message updating Alastair on his phone, indicating they were inside and attempting to retrieve the information. He left Morgan, deciding to explore a set of offices next door. He opened the locks with ease, then wandered through them, checking desks and filing cabinets along the way. He entered the last door on the right, finding a room with a large monitor and a leather chair. He searched the back of the monitor, looking for an "on" button, then pressed it. The screen flickered, the Pendragon logo emblazoned across it. He followed an AV cable from the screen to a small console on the side of the chair. Opening the top drawer, he found a hard drive imprinted with the Pendragon seal.

He flicked it on. Still nothing but the logo stared back at him. Bending over, he went through the console, finding a pair of holographic glasses. Wes examined them, then placed them on his face, the room coming alive as a 3D desktop. Data surrounded him. He spun, slightly disoriented, his hands reaching out. He moved suddenly. A file opened; his eyes widened at the content. He moved his fingers gingerly, flicking through the virtual papers in the "smear.campaign.project" file. It contained a detailed report of timed press releases to ruin the incumbent President's reputation in the next election. Wes scanned the information, shocked by the viciousness of the plan.

He moved the file aside, then typed the word Morgan. Denied in big red letters floated before him. He tried

Pendragon, then Gabby, black cat, broomstick, and other assorted words that were denied as well. His fingers typed Genevieve Fox, and the room lit up with information—most surprisingly, his own file from the bureau, as well as his father's.

"That's interesting," he murmured.

Most of the documents were reports from the field, where Genevieve Fox was employed. A former housekeeper, she had worked for a woman and two children in a small town in Nevada. Oddly enough, it was the only home in Pahrump, population 310, to have a private helipad. It was she who found the information on the President and the bigamist family he had hidden away from the public eye.

Wes read through the file, using his fingers to manipulate the words in midair. It was actually easier. He was able to twist or alternate the scrambled sentences so that his reading speed amped to a level he had never known. Once he finished with the report, he rifled through the next one, coming across one labeled "Abracadabra." It opened to images rather than reports, almost as though it were a movie.

Fuzzy sepia film stuttered, showing the world from above. He felt as though he was riding something high above the clouds at a dizzying altitude. He descended, his stomach meeting his gullet the same way as when he dropped altitude in an airplane. It was pitch black, and the stars overhead twinkled brightly.

It was close to dawn in this virtual world—he could smell the musty earthiness of early morning. Squares of white light lit up like a small patchwork on a crazy quilt of the landscape. Wes could feel the cool air as he continued his downward spiral. Looking at his legs, he noticed he was on a virtual broomstick. For a minute, he felt giddy with the unrestrained freedom of the ride. City lights flew past him. He was racing above the continental United States from the mountains sheltering California, to the middle of the country's flatlands to the rocky coastline of the East Coast. Shadows played with the brightness of the sun, painting the horizon in pink and yellow, accenting the deep canyons of the Rockies from the fertile green lands of America's breadbasket. Wes's jaw grew tight with pride. This was his country, and he was proud to wear a badge defending it. Any badge. Up here, the air was clean, as pure as untrodden snow, and just as refreshing.

He took a deep breath, forgetting it wasn't real, but allowing his lungs to feed off the imaginary oxygen. On the horizon, he could see a thin light of the sunrise, unfolding the country before him, as if drawing back a curtain. His silhouette, a lone shadow, stretched across the landscape like a banner. He pulled back, then sloped down to a closer look. Other witches patrolled the imaginary airways, but none noticed or acknowledged him. *This was Bernadette's blueprint, the very plans of her scheme,* Wes thought.

He dove low, coasting past homes and peered in the windows, looking at families eating breakfast, starting morning chores. It was peaceful and happy, the streets strangely devoid of traffic. Something was off. Wes circled back, slowing down, feeling foolish. It wasn't as though he was in a real world, just Bernadette's perception. He stopped short and moved down the suburban street again, looking closely at the families in the room. Something was wrong. All the families were missing adult males. There were no men to be found, not anywhere.

Puzzled, he rose, gaining altitude, cruising along. From his height, he noticed stadiums were lit up like shining beacons. He made a wide turn, moving lower. The fields were filled with men, living in mean barracks, merely lean-tos, devoid of heating or comfort. Huge bonfires lit open fields. Men huddled, seeking warmth. Guard towers and barbed wire enclosed the fields. Uniformed women marched outside. He gained speed, pushing to the next city, and found another ball field used the same way. Rising higher, he was able to see a giant grid of prisons, holding pens for men. It was a modern-day holocaust. *What is she planning?* Wes wondered, and a voice broke through his consciousness.

"The subjugation of the entire male population of the world."

Wes ripped off the glasses, finding himself back in the lab, the tall blonde woman from the Pendragon Headquarters watching him closely. "That's Bernadette's vision, not mine," she told him as if clarifying the information.

"It's crazy."

"I wouldn't share that with Bernadette, if I were you." She held out a graceful hand. "Give those to me." She gestured at the virtual glasses.

Wes slid them into his shirt pocket. "Morgan!" he called. He moved toward the door, calling a bit more urgently. "Morgan?"

"Oh, she can't hear you." Scarlett's sultry voice followed him. "Morgan needed a little nap."

Wes turned, his hands fisted. "If you hurt her, I'll—"

"You'll what? This is our world," Scarlett told him calmly. "You have no power here." She moved closer, so close he could feel her warm breath on his face. She reached out to walk long fingers with blood-red nails up his chest. Their eyes met. She took his inaction as an invitation to run her hands up and down his chest possessively.

"I like you, delivery boy." She licked her lips. "I could make things better for you," she whispered close to his ear. "You won't have to go to an internment camp. You'll stay with me." Her eyes gleamed feverishly in the dimly lit room.

Wes pushed her away, disgust written plainly on his face.

"Oh, you doubt our power, don't you? All you men think

you are so strong. Invincible. While you've been building your empires, making us second-class citizens, we've been busy building our own." Her eyes narrowed to tight slits.

"Who says you're second-class citizens?" Wes demanded.

"As witches, our type has been oppressed for years. We are not allowed to do what we want, but that's the tip of the iceberg." Scarlett warmed to her subject. She spun away from him, caught up in her anger.

"You're insane. Women won't follow you!"

"Think again. They have been deprived of equal pay and equal respect, for too long!" She punched a fist in the air. "This will shatter the glass ceiling. What do you know about equality?" She sneered.

Wes swallowed hard. Seems he did know a lot about shame, about feeling unequal to people who could read with the same effort as breathing. He knew persecution, of being passed over because of a disability or being invisible in a family photo as though he were inferior.

"If you do this, you are no better than the people you accuse of oppressing you." He backed out of the room to find Morgan floating in midair, her face serene, a green haze surrounding her.

Wes pulled out his Darrow Trance Lifter, aiming it at Morgan. He pressed the control. Behind him, Scarlett laughed. "That won't work in this building, fool. Bernadette has protected her compound. None of your silly toys function here."

Scarlett came up behind him, wrapping her arms around his midsection, rubbing her body against his. Wes turned abruptly to grab her shoulders, shaking her. Her blonde hair flew around her face. She looked up, her eyes smoky. "Like it rough, do you?" She laughed.

Wes released her as if she'd singed him. "Let her go."

Scarlett's laughter ricocheted off the walls. "Why? What are you going to do about it? Here, you're in my universe! Look at me!" She spun around, her eyes hot and glowing. "Morgan's a twit. She doesn't know how to please a man."

Wes's eyes raked her body with a smirk. "And you think you do?"

Wes could feel the vibration of Scarlet's anger; the room hummed with it. Balling her fists, she stared at him. All around him, machinery started to smoke. Small explosions sounded as beakers shattered. Computers lit up, whining with life.

"What are you trying to prove?" he mocked her.

"Scarlett. Say my name. It's Scarlett!" Wind swirled around him, sending papers flying. A burst of static electrified the room.

A cat screeched. Wes knew Luna had escaped; her cry became fainter. "No," he told her flatly.

Scarlett's lips firmed. Making a fist, she threw something at him, which bounced off his chest harmlessly. He felt another impact on his shoulder. He started moving purposely toward her. Scarlett opened eager arms, then cursed loudly as he brushed past her and approached Morgan. He wrapped his arms around the floating girl's inert form, trying to spin her into a standing position. This time, an impact to the middle of his back stung, sending him colliding with Morgan. He refused to acknowledge Scarlett. When the next one smashed into his head, his vision went black for a moment.

"Don't ignore me!" Scarlett shouted.

"Or what? I don't like you."

Scarlett's face turned red with fury. She ran to him, colliding with his body, sending them into a bank of filing cabinets. "You're stupid. You have no future with her." She hit him. He deflected her fists easily. "She's ugly."

"You've got to be kidding me. Do you have a magic mirror like Bags?" he taunted.

Scarlett screamed, smacking him in the face. "You're dead, if I say so. You don't understand. I am going to be the one. Bernadette is going to leave everything to me. To me! That whey-faced creep is going down. Morgan can't have you. She can't have anything. I am going to have it all." Scarlett flicked her tongue, her eyes opening in shock when Wes recoiled with disgust.

He backed away, asking her, "Do you hiss like a snake, too?"

This time, she allowed her tongue to tease him. It moved in a sensuous dance around her lush lips, its forked tips shivering with need. "What's the matter, you don't like my tongue? Double the pleasure." She put her finger near her mouth, wrapping her serpent's tongue around it suggestively.

"You're a troll," Wes said through gritted teeth.

"Have you ever seen a troll? A real one?" she asked, her voice seductive. "We'll have to revisit this later. Perhaps a threesome. You, me, and a troll I know. Let's see what you think then."

Scarlett spun, her eyes fastening on a stapler. She stabbed her index finger at it. It rose, firing off staples like a machine gun while she muttered, "Staples, staples, do not maul, just attach him to the wall."

Moments later, Wes found himself splayed on the wall of the lab, his shirt and pants fastened by staples. He tried to move but was held fast. Scarlett walked past him, running her hands possessively down his immobile leg. "That was easy," she said with a snicker. "I'll be back for you later, and if you cooperate, you won't end up in an internment camp. Maybe you'll grow to enjoy troll rolls." She flicked her tongue at him.

Wes struggled, but the staples wouldn't move. "You won't get away with this."

"Watch me."

"Morgan!" Wes shouted.

Scarlett ripped a length of tape and levitated so that she was eyeball-to-eyeball with him. She leaned forward, her lips inches from his. Wes moved his face away, but she grabbed his chin with relentless fingers. Her mouth covered his for a kiss. "I'm kinda stuck on you," she told him with a laugh, then sealed his lips with tape. "I'll be back for you later."

Scarlett took out her phone, punching in a number. "Yeah," she said, "I'm heading there right now. No, I haven't seen Morgan." She slid her phone back into her bag. "And neither will you, Bernadette," she said to herself. "She'll be at the bottom of Red Hook's harbor."

Wes called out impotently, his voice muffled by the tape. Scarlett walked out of the room, Morgan, oblivious, floating behind her. He watched a clock ticking in the corner, cursing Luna and her escape. She might have been able to help in some way.

It felt like hours later that the tape was ripped from Wes's lips.

"Why are you hanging around?" Alastair quipped, using a staple remover to free Wes.

"Okay, I believe in witches now," Wes told him as he hopped down. "Where's Junie?"

"They took her downtown to give a statement. What happened?"

"Scarlett took Morgan. They are headed for Red Hook. You won't believe what they have planned. How'd you get in here?"

"Bribed the guard. How did you?"

"We just hopped right in." They got into Alastair's SUV, racing toward the Brooklyn ports. On the way, Wes recounted what he'd found in Bernadette's private file. "This whole thing can't be real. They'll never be able to do it," Wes said when he finished telling the story.

"What makes you think it can't happen? Sometimes the truth is stranger than science fiction. History is filled with mass killings, enslavements, genocides, going back throughout time. Pick a time period, Wes. In the Messenian Wars, ancient Sparta reduced the entire population to slavery, so that slaves outnumbered the Spartans seven to one. Rome enslaved most of Europe, building an empire that spanned the continent. While the British didn't support slavery at home, they condoned it throughout their empire, creating a vile economy based on slave trade. Slave labor kept the German machine running during the Second World War. Sorry, Wes," Alastair said shaking his head, "the idea of enslavement is not as far-fetched as it sounds."

"That can't happen here!" Wes exclaimed.

"Two weeks ago, you didn't believe in witches. What will it take for you to understand that freedom is fragile? We must never forget what man, or woman, is capable of? That's the reason we protect these women and their right to practice."

"Willas can use the same argument just as easily. They believe they have those rights, too."

"Look, we can spend a lifetime debating the subject. Every person should have the right to practice and believe what they want as long as it does not infringe on another person's freedom."

"I'm sure Bernadette Pendragon is convinced she is a crusader for a just cause," Wes said. "I always said you have to get the hydra at the head."

Alastair slowed, his face whitening with a sudden realization. Holding up a finger, he paused the conversation. "We're going to have to split up."

"What?" Wes questioned.

"Call for backup. Get out of the car," Alastair said, pulling onto the shoulder of the Brooklyn Queens Expressway.

Vehicles whizzed past them on the highway. Over the roar of the cars, Wes shouted, "You can't leave me here!"

"They'll be here in five minutes to pick you up. I'll meet you in Red Hook," Alastair responded.

"Where are you going?"

"Pendragon."

CHAPTER NINETEEN

Morgan floated three feet off the ground, trailing behind Scarlett, who hummed absently. Scarlett pointed two fingers to the lock on the door and watched it sizzle as the entrance to the warehouse in Red Hook opened. Scarlett snapped on the lights as they walked. She looked with satisfaction at the towers of containers holding millions of packs of Pendragon Glow.

Scarlett turned, waving her arm. Morgan landed with a crash onto the concrete, the green haze gone. Morgan rolled over, rubbing the shoulder that took the brunt of the fall.

"What is going on, Scarlett? Where are we?" Morgan looked around at the unfamiliar surroundings.

"I'd like nothing more than to make you disappear." Scarlett sniffed.

"I'm not signing those papers." Morgan rose angrily.

"You think this is about you?" Scarlett laughed, walking around Morgan. "You little pest. You are always in the way. Scarlett, get Morgan a latte. Scarlett, take Morgan's dry cleaning out. Scarlett, wipe Morgan's skinny ass." She stopped to stare hard at the younger girl. "I hate you!" Scarlett clapped her hands and rolled them.

A force tugged Morgan, lifting her and tossing her like wet laundry against a metal container. She hit it with a thud, then slid to the floor. Scarlett motioned again, and Morgan was thrown across the room, crashing into a plastic drum. Black dots swam before her eyes. Morgan reached feebly for her willow wand in her pocket.

"Looking for this, bitch?" Scarlett held up the thin branch Morgan had taken off the tree in New Jersey. "Pretty weak, just like you." Scarlett dropped it on the floor, using the ball of her foot to grind it into pulp. "That's what I want to do to you," she sneered.

"Stop," Morgan said weakly.

"I want to be her favorite! Why should you have all the luck? What accident of birth gives you the right to have it better than me?" Scarlett screamed, her face mottled red, a vein bulging on her neck.

Scarlett whirled, sending Morgan spinning high. She twirled Morgan faster and faster, so the room turned muddy. Nausea rose in Morgan's throat. Try as she might, she couldn't squeeze the words out. Scarlett slammed her hand. Morgan fell with terrifying speed, staring dully at the floor, thinking this would end it all, when Scarlett halted her with a sickening stop inches above the concrete. The blonde bent over Morgan's bruised body, her face inches from her own. "Do you know the best part of being a witch?"

Morgan ignored her. Her head throbbed; everything hurt.

Scarlett grabbed her chin, forcing her to look at her. "No fingerprints." Scarlett threaded her cold hands around Morgan's neck, a gentle caress that tightened so the girl thrashed help-lessly trying to pry off the strangling fingers.

A male voice interrupted Scarlett. "Excuse me, miss. Excuse

me." The lights around her hummed to life as the entire warehouse lit up.

Looking up, she released the hold she had on Morgan, who
she dropped to the floor in a boneless heap.

"Is there a problem here?" a long-nosed, potbellied man
persisted.

"Do you mind? I'm a little busy," Scarlett told him.

The little man advanced into the room, followed by a crew
of burly longshoremen. "As a matter of fact, I do mind. You got
no business here and, being this is our dock, you can't whack
somebody without asking."

"Can I use your space to whack her?"

Dominic, the dock boss, thought for a minute, his finger by
his mouth. He looked Scarlett straight in the eye and replied,
"Uh ... no."

"Look, Pinocchio. I'm going to count to three." Scarlett
stood, Morgan forgotten, to face the short man and his crew.
"One ..."

Dominic folded his arms over his puny chest. Two men
appeared at his side, twelve-gauge shotguns pumped and ready.

Morgan scrambled to her feet, inching toward a long
alleyway of containers.

"Two ..." Scarlett's voice was low, the men's eyes riveted
on her.

Morgan slipped down the narrow passageway, ducking
behind the metal boxes to find a hideaway. Scarlett turned to
look for her, cursing under her breath when she realized she was
gone.

"Three." Scarlett raised her hands, palms forward, the shotguns making a ninety-degree bend to aim at the ceiling.

"You're a witch!" Dominic shouted.

"No shit, Sherlock," Scarlett replied, pointing to a container
thirty feet high. "Box them in, seal the door, ship them all to

Singapore." The rectangular box fell with a crash and opened like a grapefruit. The men rolled into the center. The box resealed instantly. There was the sizzle of something burning, and a shipping label appeared on the outside. Fists pounded futilely from inside. Dominic screamed furiously that Ms. Pendragon was going to hear about this.

Scarlett turned to the vast cavern of the warehouse, the drumming from the men imprisoned in the metal box becoming fainter as she walked the aisles. "Hey, hey, oh playmate," she began in a singsong voice. "Come out and play with me. You'll bring your dollies three. Climb up my apple tree …" Her voice had a breathy quality that echoed down the deserted warehouse. "Slide down my rain barrel. Into my cellar door …"

Morgan's foot slipped. The singing stopped abruptly. Scarlett's eyes widened, an evil smile on her face. She wet her lips, beginning the song again. "And we'll be jolly friends …" Scarlett tossed aside a heavy container with her bare hands, her mouth a snarl as she finished the childhood ditty, expecting to find her prey. "Forever more!" Morgan wasn't there. Scarlett sniffed the air; she knew the girl was nearby. "Come out, come out, wherever you are. I won't hurt you, Morgan. I love you … like the sister I never had."

Morgan hung onto the back of a corrugated container, her breath frozen in her throat.

CHAPTER TWENTY

Wes jumped out of the replacement car before it even stopped, the gravel of the dock spewing as the tires squealed. His badge hanging from his neck, he surveyed the scene. Black cars surrounded the warehouse in Red Hook, red and blue lights flashing. Uniformed men holding assault rifles crouched in the darkness. His driver pointed to a van with the doors open—an impromptu command post. Three men stood together consulting blueprints of the building, their backs to Wes.

Wes couldn't miss the bald head of his father anywhere. Harris Rockville stood in the center, listening intently to another man with a peaked hat. He nodded, his hand on his large jaw, his eyes intense.

"Dad?" Wes ran up.

Harris nodded, but spoke to the other man. "I want that corner locked down. Make sure the snipers have a clear shot." He pointed to a building across the way. "Four snipers up there. We'll go with three teams inside."

"Dad, what are you doing here?"

The two men ran off, leaving father and son alone. "We'll take over from here."

"Like hell you will!" Wes answered hotly.

"One screw-up on the job is enough. You lost the girl."

"No, I didn't. She's here, and I'll get her out!" Wes shouted, pointing to the warehouse.

Harris gestured his second in command to approach him, then pointed to Wes. "Get him off the premises."

"Excuse me," a female voice trilled, interrupting the unfolding drama. "I need to find Agent Rockville."

Both Wes and his father turned to see Junie approach them from the darkness.

"Who let you in here?" Harris demanded rudely.

"Nobody. I have a card," Junie smiled sweetly, showing her entry ID for the gate. "Hi, Wes," she said, eyeing the bruise on his forehead. "Oh, nasty bump there. I have something for it." She reached into her large carpetbag.

"You know this person?" His father turned to him, his face furious.

"Yes." Wes was breathing hard. "This is Junie 'Bags' Meadows. Junie, this is my father, Agent Harris Rockville."

Harris faced her, a smile spreading across his face. He held out his hand. "Junie 'Bags' Meadows, it's an honor. I've heard so much about you."

"The honor is mine," Junie said coyly. "Well, I can certainly see where those big blue eyes come from."

"We have to get in there and cancel the Pendragon shipment," Wes told Junie. He turned to his father. "She knows where the manifests are."

Harris spoke to his team. "Get ready to move in."

"You can't go in there guns blazing. Morgan is being held there!"

"Stand down, Agent Rockville!" his father ordered.

"With all due respect, sir, this is a category-seven witch we are dealing with," Wes informed him.

Harris looked at him intently. "Son. I've been dealing with witches since before you were born. Everything I know I learned in the Witches Protection Program. Alastair was my first partner. Why do you think I placed you there? But now it's time for you to stand down and let me take over."

"Dad ..."

"Good night, Wes." He spun to his agents. "Team six, move! Junie, after you." Junie followed them in. The shadow of a cat trailed unnoticed behind her.

CHAPTER TWENTY-ONE

A lastair, clad all in black, entered the Pendragon tower through the basement where the trash was collected. Dashing up six levels, he sprinted through the silent lobby, his feet barely touching the marble. He moved stealthily to the service elevator, pressing the button, waiting patiently to reach the penthouse.

The door opened to the back of Bernadette's darkened office, the city skyline illuminating her pale face. Bernadette faced the window. Her eyes were on the distant ports, the large ships weighted down with containers of her face cream.

"You're too late, Alastair," she said without turning around.

"Better late than never," Alastair responded quietly.

Bernadette turned. She was smoking a cigarette. The ember was long, hanging like an orange inchworm glowing in the dark. "Where's Morgan?" she asked wearily.

"I don't know. Ask Scarlett." He walked into the room.

Bernadette turned, her face, shocked. "Scarlett? What are you talking about?"

"Scarlett kidnapped her. She probably has her in a container heading for Timbuktu by now."

"Stupid, stupid girls." Bernadette ground out her cigarette. "They don't know how to do anything these days. And they call themselves witches?" She laughed hollowly. "Anyway, Morgan probably deserves it. She hasn't done anything right." She walked languidly to her desk, picking up the largest red stone. She hefted it from hand to hand.

"And you have?"

"You dare to question me?" Bernadette placed both her hands on her desk, the stone underneath her palm.

Alastair shrugged. "This has got to stop," he said simply.

"Here you go again, always trying to right the wrong. Well, who says I was wrong?" It was clear they weren't talking about anything taking place now.

"Catarina did."

Bernadette walked around her desk to come face-to-face with him, her hands fisted by her side. "Catarina was a coward."

"You'll have to live a thousand lifetimes to catch up to her bravery and loyalty."

"Spare me the clichéd movie lines!" Bernadette snapped.

Alastair held up a sheaf of papers. "I have a warrant for your arrest."

Bernadette stared hard at the file, her eyes turning into yellow blazes of light. Flames burst from the papers, licking Alastair's fingers. He dropped them onto the carpet, stamping on them. "Don't show off."

"I loved you!" Bernadette wailed.

"And I loved your sister," Alastair answered quickly.

Bernadette approached him, her face stark. "Why didn't you want me?" She tried to take his hand, but he pulled away.

Alastair looked her full in the face. "Because you are pure, unadulterated evil."

"There is a fine line between good and evil, Alastair," Bernadette told him coldly. "It's called perspective."

"You have no soul," Alastair said sadly.

"Stop blaming me! It was not my fault!" Bernadette screamed. "The accident was not my fault." She threw the rock at the window, which bounced harmlessly to the floor.

"It's over, Bernadette," Alastair told her.

Bernadette spun, holding a small gun in her thin, white hand. "It's not over until I say so."

CHAPTER TWENTY-TWO

Junie stood in Dominic's office, surrounded by Harris's team. They pored over the files, boxing the documents they ripped from the drawers. She typed her password, opening the manifests and muttered, "Damn."

Tapping again at the keyboard, she repeated her profanity, causing Harris to come over and gaze over her shoulder to read her screen.

Junie shook her head. "It's too late. The ships left port hours ago. They hid the manifests under different names."

Harris's blue eyes scanned the documents. "It still says the containers are here."

"That's what I'm telling you. It's an old trick." Junie paused at his expression. "Well, it is. See?" She pointed her bony finger at a list. "These five ships all have the products." She typed again. "They've put it under Comstock Industries, which is …" She typed some more. "… a shell for Pendragon." Junie turned to look at the agent. "She must have smelled something. They really had to hustle to get that stuff out of here."

Harris punched the keyboard, combing the manifests.

Luna meowed loudly and jumped onto the desk. Junie rubbed her face into the dark fur affectionately. She opened her carpetbag for the cat to slide in.

"Rockville, you need to see this." A uniformed agent poked his head in the office.

Harris turned to his second in command. "Get the Coast Guard involved. Call Washington. I'll be right back."

He rushed down the steps, following his man to a container that had been pried open. Four longshoremen and an overweight office worker sat on the floor, blankets covering them, water bottles in their hands. One man was propped against the wall of the metal container, breathing hard. Misshapen shotguns, their barrels twisted upward, lay on the floor next to them.

"Dominic Cerillo, manager of the building," the agent relayed.

"Are they hurt?"

The man shrugged. "Dehydrated, scared. I don't know if they are more terrified of that blonde witch or us."

"What'd you get?" Harris asked his associate.

"They've been here since yesterday, pushing out the Pendragon order on the down-low. It's gone, sir, and I don't think we are going to be able to intercept. According to Dominic here"—he pointed to the man who seemed to shrink before his eyes—"they are probably in international waters already."

Harris cursed. "What else?"

"This way." They left the container to move to one farther down the lane. "A girl. She was tied up. I've got a medic—"

"I get the picture," Harris said, approaching Morgan.

She was rubbing her reddened wrist. The girl paused, holding out a hand to Harris. "Morgan Pendragon. I wish I could say it is a pleasure to meet you."

Harris took her cold hand in his own. "Are you all right?"

"No thanks to that stupid agent Wes Rockville. I've seen Keystone Cops that are more professional," she spat.

Harris winced, grinding his teeth. "Sorry, miss. What did he do, exactly?"

"The man's an idiot. He doesn't follow orders, thinks he knows everything … oh, never mind. You should be looking for that Scarlett woman. She did this to me, and he let her!"

"Fan out!" Harris ordered. "Colon, Hornik, take that corridor." He pointed to a dimly lit passageway. "Glass, Wasserman, you take the left. Can you tell us what she looks like?"

"She's beautiful. Tall, blonde, and very lethal," Morgan responded.

The men turned sideways, walking slowly, guns drawn, looking for the blonde perpetrator.

"Follow me, if you don't mind, Miss Pendragon. I need to fill out a report." Harris took her by the elbow, guiding her toward the front of the building, his mind on his incompetent son. *Jeez*, he thought, *where did I go wrong with that one?* As if he'd conjured him up, he heard a rising voice.

"I told you to leave," Harris said angrily. "Wes!" Harris pointed to an officer. "I told you to take him out of here."

The officer pulled his gun as he walked purposefully toward Wes.

Wes looked at Morgan. His face closed up, his smile vanished, and his expression became hostile. He abruptly turned to run down a narrow corridor, his breathing harsh, his face wet with sweat. His father's gruff voice called after him, but he concentrated on separating the different sounds echoing through the warehouse. He paused at an intersection, listening to the scuffle of feet. He screamed, "Morgan!" His heart raced. A faint sound, metal against metal, traveled down the passage. Wes ran, his feet flying, stopping at corners to gauge the direction. "Left, left … no, right, right," he whispered. "Morgan!" he called out again, the answering clatter pushing him to the last row. He banged hard against the metal walls, his fists stinging. Pulling open the first giant box, he found it stacked with product. He called her name again, relieved when he heard the rap of her response. *The next one.* He yanked it open. Morgan fell into his arms, breathless. He pushed the hair back from her damp face, kissing her full on the lips. Hot tears bathed her face. She pressed it against his shoulder, relief making her weak. Her slight body sagged against him. Holding her away, he asked, "Can you walk?"

"We've got to get out of here. Scarlett, she's deranged."

Wes took her hand, walking briskly back to the entrance. Pulling out his cell, he pressed his father's number. It went directly to voicemail. "Dad, call me."

He punched it again, but this time there was no service. Panic swelled in his chest. Picking up his pace, he started running, Morgan dragging behind him.

Relief flooded Wes as they broke out into the entrance. His father stood in the frame of the big doors, his face livid. "Just what in the hell …" The words died on Harris's lips when he realized his son held the hand of a very winded Morgan Pendragon. Twisting, he registered Wes's shout as bullets exploded from a gun, snatched from the officer next to the fake Morgan. Wes shouted but grabbed the real Morgan, rolling with her on the filthy floor, then covering her with his body.

Scarlett shot wildly, her face in a feral snarl. "You!" she sneered, walking toward Wes. Aiming directly at his head, she squeezed the trigger, hearing nothing but a click. Before Wes could look up, she flew over him, disappearing into the darkness of the warehouse. A few shots were fired from the startled police. Wes waved at them to halt.

"Stop. You're not equipped correctly. Those won't do

anything to her." He ran to his father's prone body, but the sound of distant gunfire called. Saying a silent farewell, he exchanged a pained look with Morgan, who struggled to her feet. "Stay here," he ordered, then took off into the darkness behind them.

Wes pulled his Steampunk revolver, his thumb flicking open the lever that warmed the glowing liquid in the ammunition chamber. The weapon hummed with heat, a high-pitched whine letting him know it was ready.

His back hugging the corrugated metal, he walked slowly, his eyes scanning the top for the blonde witch. Something dropped. He rushed into the next aisle to find nothing but a black corridor yawning before him. A door opened with a creak, then slammed. Wes turned around to see Scarlett standing in front of him, hands on her hips.

"Hello, handsome. Dump the bitch?"

Wes extended his arm, pointing the gun directly at her.

"Go ahead, shoot an unarmed woman."

Wes squeezed the trigger, recoiling at the impact, a stream of green foam shooting toward his target. Scarlett's laughter filled the void.

"Didn't you practice with that thing?"

Wes turned, and found her behind him. He aimed again. The gun flew from his hands to land on the concrete in front of her.

"You can't hurt me with that popgun."

"What about this one?" Harris yelled, pointing an Aether cannon directly at her. "Down, Wes!" he shouted. Wes dove, but Scarlett spun into a starburst that disintegrated into a glittering explosion.

"Dad!" Wes rose, running to him. "Are you okay?"

Harris lifted his shirt, showing his bulletproof vest. "What happened to her?"

"Not sure, but you didn't get off a shot."

They heard a scuffle toward the front of the building. They both took off, only to find the entrance floor littered with dazed police.

"Morgan?" Wes called.

"She took her. She swooped in and flew off with her," an officer said from the floor.

"Where did she go?" Harris asked.

"I know," Wes said.

Harris looked at his son. "Then go get her."

CHAPTER TWENTY-THREE

P lease keep both arms and legs at your sides during takeoffs and landings," Scarlett laughed. She had Morgan in front of her on a purloined push broom as they circled the Pendragon helipad. Scarlett hovered four feet off the ground, then abruptly pushed Morgan off the broom. "Oops, I suppose you're going to ask for a refund."

Scarlett gracefully glided to the tarmac, landing neatly. The door opened, and Alastair walked out, his hands held up in front of him. Behind him, Bernadette prodded him forward with a small handgun. Her book of spells was tucked under her arm.

"What are you doing here?" Bernadette demanded, her eyes raking Morgan, then Scarlett.

"Oh," Scarlett said sarcastically, "a family reunion."

"What's going on?"

"Your little niece here tried to stop the shipments. She led the authorities there. I had the foresight to move the shipments this morning. If not for me, your cream would be rotting on the docks."

"What about his partner?" Bernadette gestured to Alastair.

"Dead. I took care of him."

"Look." Alastair felt his eyes fill. He turned to Bernadette. "It's over. You've won. Let the girl go."

Bernadette looked at Morgan, then turned on Alastair contemptuously. "What a good daddy. You don't even know her." She pounded her thin chest. "I raised her!"

Alastair spun, his face a mask of grief. "That was your choice. You took my choice when you killed Catarina!"

Morgan sat on the ground, stunned. She whispered, "What?" She looked at Bernadette, her dark eyes sunken, her face drained of color.

Bernadette held her hands in front of her, almost forgetting she held a weapon. "It was an accident."

"There's no such thing as an accident when dealing with a Willa," Alastair responded scornfully.

"You only wanted her …" Bernadette said to Alastair. "I didn't understand why. We were the same—only you wouldn't look at me."

"What did you do?" Morgan demanded, standing close to her. "What did you do?"

"We were driving home. It was a little spell, only a little one. There was an oncoming car. She was supposed to … I didn't mean for her to get killed. I read it in my book. It went, 'Your eyes are heavy, you don't see the car, hit us so my sister will scar.' You see, it was an accident. I'll show you. It's here in the book." She held out the tattered book to her niece.

"You killed my mother!" Morgan screamed.

"It was an accident. Only her face was supposed to be hurt. The spell went wrong, Morgan." Bernadette looked at Alastair. "You were supposed to want *me*."

Morgan turned to Wes's partner as though she had just noticed he was there. "What is she talking about?"

"Your mother and I …"

"No …" Morgan backed away from him.

Alastair shook his head sadly. "I loved your mother. We were married. You were heir to your mother's portion of the Pendragon empire. After the … accident, Bernadette wanted me, but I couldn't look at her. I knew what she had done. You were supposed to be with me, Morgan, but she swore she would kill you too if I didn't give her total custody. I'm sorry, but I can't fight her magic." He reached out, but she tore her hands away. "I had no choice. She changed your name to Pendragon and purged me from your life."

Morgan looked at them both through a veil of tears. "You gave me away …"

"I never wanted to," Alastair said quietly.

"I don't believe you."

"I joined the Witches Protection Program so I could learn how to protect you. It was all for you. I've been waiting for this moment for a long time."

The door to the helipad cracked. Wes stood in the entrance, listening to Morgan's sobs.

"How could you?" Morgan turned on Bernadette.

"How dare you?" Bernadette demanded, her face white. "I raised you as though you were my own. I did all this for you! I sacrificed my life for you!"

"All you ever cared about was power," Morgan shot back. "You don't love me; you don't love anybody but yourself. You just want to control me. If you really did this for me, you wouldn't insist I sign those papers giving up everything."

"It was all for you!" Bernadette insisted. "You're too stupid to comprehend, just like your mother. She didn't understand either. Dutiful Davinas. Let's create pretty makeup to let women feel good about themselves. Let's fix the sick. Let's donate money. For whom? For what? Women do all that for men, who hold the real power, and they get nothing in return. It's our time now! Men will be our slaves and do what we want."

"I don't want to listen to this!" Morgan held her hands over her ears, her face awash with tears.

"It is your birthright!" Bernadette threw her book of spells at Morgan, hitting her squarely in the chest. It bounced off her and landed on the ground, the pages fluttering in the wind.

"Stop. This is madness! You have no right to do this," Morgan told her. "I don't want any part of you."

"It's over, Bernadette. Look at her. She hates you. It's time to stop," Alastair said.

Bernadette levitated, her arms spread wide, her eyes hard, gray marbles ignoring them all. "I will control everyone. No more bleeding-heart Davinas! No more witch hunters! No more persecution of my kind!"

"The way to end persecution is to not repeat the offense," Alastair told her.

Bernadette continued as though she hadn't heard. "All the individuals who suppressed us, kept us in our place, and frightened us will be under my dominion! My will *will* prevail!" She circled Alastair and Morgan. "The world will bow to me! To me!" Her laughter echoed down the streets of Manhattan.

Turning to Scarlett, she held out her long-fingered hand to her. "Join me, Scarlett, my loyal one. You've always been there for me, haven't you? Silent and steady, my right arm. Join me. Let's finish this together."

Wes burst through the door, launching himself at Bernadette's dangling feet. He passed Morgan, his foot landing on the book, ripping the pages so that they caught on the wind, flying off the top of the building.

Bernadette angrily watched the pages of her book wafting in the air. They were gone. She didn't have the time to retrieve them. "I thought you said he was dead." Bernadette glared at

Scarlett. Her hand rotated, producing an ice ball, which she threw at Wes.

Both Morgan and Alastair saw him. Morgan started running to him, crying, "Wes!" She only knew she needed to feel the safety of his arms.

Scarlett pushed her back, saying, "I'll get him."

Bernadette grabbed Scarlett by the hair, pulling her head backward, her face twisted. "You incompetent twit. You've ruined everything! Watch me do it."

"Get down, Wes!" Alastair called, pulling Morgan with him and sprinting to duck behind the boxlike generators.

Wes stood tall, walking intently toward Bernadette, his glowing revolver in his steady hand. "My name is Wesley Rockville." An ice ball flew close to his face. He bent backward, avoiding it. "I'm an agent with the Witches Protection Program."

Bernadette lobbed a flurry of ice balls, now encased in fire. One grazed his shoulder, scorching his shirt, but he didn't stop his single-minded determination to reach her. Pages from her book became plastered against his body. Bernadette screamed in frustration, pitching an ice ball that hit him full in the stomach. Wes went down, rolling to the edge of the building, his weapon flying from his hand when he hit the floor.

Morgan's quick intake of breath revealed their spot. Alastair pulled his revolver from his ankle holster, aiming at Bernadette. The gun ejected from his hands, sliding to the middle of the helipad from a roundhouse kick to his jaw from Scarlett, now hovering over them. He reached for his Trance Lifter. Scarlett snatched it, throwing it into the center of the helipad, laughing. "What else have you got, old man?" She kicked him again, and he went down like a stone.

Morgan leaped onto Scarlett, who backed her into the generator, causing sparks to fly into the dark night. Scarlett grabbed Morgan's head with both hands and banged it on the metal box. Morgan slid senseless to the ground, a line of blood on her forehead.

To Alastair's groggy surprise, the blonde woman now turned to her mentor. "You can't minimize me! This is my company! This is my fortune! I wasn't some witch's bitch for five years to become your personal assistant. I will be bigger than you, Bernadette! I will be bigger than you!" she repeated, her face contorted with rage.

Wes crawled toward Bernadette, determination written on his face. Alastair slid his lasso chain from the back of his jacket. One shot—Scarlett or Bernadette? He waffled, and Scarlett's fingertips darted at him with a blaze of light, incapacitating him. She winked out of sight.

Bernadette waved her arms in giant circles, gathering a maelstrom of energy. Baring her teeth, she grunted, aiming her deadly attack on Wes.

Wes watched a giant ball of icy fire head toward him. His gun was lying in the middle of the helipad next to Alastair's. Backed against the wall, he felt something hard in his pocket. Reaching in, he slid out the small compact. "You'll know when to use it," Alastair had told him. *It seems as good a time as any,* he thought. He was out of any other alternatives, anyway. Touching the lever with the pad of his thumb, the clamshell opened. He turned it to the oncoming fireball. The heat of the flames singed his flesh. The ice ball hung for a second in midair, then, its direction reversing, it rolled backward, smacking Bernadette in the face and covered her with a gel-like substance. Bernadette screamed, the sound echoing off the rooftop, her hands covering her face, skin bubbling underneath her fingers.

Alastair stood on rubbery legs, swinging his lasso feebly to Wes. "She's all yours. Don't be fooled; she's quite dangerous," he called.

Bernadette stumbled backward, away from Wes, falling on her knees.

Wes caught the device, snapping it. "How does this thing …?" The lasso surprised Bernadette, wrapping around her waist, but instead of reeling her in, the chain towed Wes to her with amazing speed. Bending, he scooped up Alastair's revolver as he was dragged past it, pushing it into the back of his pants, while his feet desperately fought to gain purchase on the helipad.

Bernadette faltered, backing to the edge of the building until her heels slid off. Wes saw her waver and reached forward to grab her, but they both toppled off the helipad, plummeting toward the street below. The chain that connected them caught on a flagpole, hooking them so they were dangling on either side. Wes held on, his bleeding hands wrapped around the metal chain. He looked at Bernadette, recoiling at her skull-like features. Her skin festered, making her look like an ancient crone. "You have the right to remain silent," he told her, breathless but determined. "Anything you say or do can and will be used against you in—"

"You have got to be kidding me," Bernadette said. Kicking out, she launched herself into a window behind her, shattering it and leaving both Wes and the lasso chain dangling from the sixtieth floor.

Wes cursed loudly as the chain began to slide with no counterbalance to hold him there. Reaching out, he grabbed it with his other hand, feeling it shred the flesh of his palms. Using his weight, he inched his way to the shattered window. Swinging back and forth to gain momentum, he leaped through the glass, landing with a crunch on a bed of broken shards.

Bernadette's wails filled the room. She turned, her face a bloody mess. "Look what you've done to me!" she screamed. "Look at me! Look at me!"

"Fool me once, shame on you; fool me twice—"

"Look at my eyes," she urged. The yellow glow filled the room.

Wes shielded his face. "You can't control me. I have my free will."

He heard Bernadette snap her fingers.

Wind blew all around him, buffeting him. He was lifted off his feet and blown around, his skin tingling. He felt like he was in the center of a tornado. Wes closed his eyes, nausea overtaking him. He finally opened his eyes to find himself back on the helipad. Alastair was frozen, covered with ice.

Bernadette was kneeling, exhausted, her yellow, blazing eyes a beacon that Wes refused to look at.

Scarlett stood in the center, her hands emitting a blue light that encased Morgan, rolled into a frozen ball, hanging suspended in midair.

Alastair floated next to her in the same blue cloud, his beard making him look like a hip version of Father Frost.

Scarlett rose above them. "I am the CEO. I am the Board of Directors. I am the Almighty. I am the most powerful witch. I will control everything! I will disperse *my* DNA! I am the sorceress and the center of this earth!" She turned her palms to face Wes.

Lethargy enveloped Wes. Ice crystallized on his skin. Numbly, he watched his vision darken; he heard his own heartbeat slow. Something pulled him. He noticed dully that he was on the edge of the building again, next to Morgan.

Bernadette looked up. "No," she said weakly, inching toward the Trance Lifter. Picking it up, she aimed it at Scarlett. "Not my child," she said, and Wes wondered if she meant Morgan or her empire.

The beam caught Scarlett in the chest. Her spell vanished instantly, throwing her backward to land on her bottom. The blue haze surrounding Alastair, Morgan, and Wes faded at the same time. Wes reached for Morgan but lost his balance. They teetered in a macabre dance, then fell into the blackness.

Bernadette dragged herself to the edge of the building, screaming despairingly, "Nooo! Morgan!" Then she called out, "Use your damn powers! Fly, damn you."

Bernadette's wail cut through the night sky, rousing Morgan. She peered up, her eyes locking on her aunt. "Use your powers. If not for you, then for him." She pointed to Wes. Wes was below her, looking up, his face stark.

Closing her eyes, Morgan searched for a spell. She knew she had to find one fast. She didn't have a wand. She leveled out next to Wes, wanting nothing more than to have his arms around her. As if he read her thoughts, Wes reached out, his fingers grazing her. They touched, and spangles of bright light sparked from her fingers, the words coming out of her mouth without a thought. "Let me soar, with my love, give us flight, just like a dove." The air thickened. Their descent slowed as if they were cocooned in soft wool. Their arms surrounded each other and they bounced as if they were buoyantly catching waves in the ocean. Morgan smiled triumphantly. Wes laughed out loud. He reached to carry her.

"I'm really sorry about this, but I think it will be the only way," Morgan told him, the wind ruffling her hair. Placing her hands under his knees, she lifted him up with a burst that took them to the top of the building.

Bernadette turned to a pasty-faced Alastair. "She can fly!" she said triumphantly.

Alastair closed his eyes with relief. "Wes?"

"Safe. They'll be here in a minute. So will your team. They've surrounded the building." They both looked at Scarlett's crumpled form. "All I ever wanted was you," she told him simply.

Alastair looked at her ravaged beauty, shaking his head. "No, you didn't. You wanted to control me. When you couldn't, you went after the rest of the male population."

"A girl's gotta do what a girl's gotta do."

The door to the helipad opened, disgorging a team of agents. They surrounded the prone body of the blonde witch, placing tape over her mouth, tying her hands with chain, and finally covering her face with burlap.

Harris and another agent approached Bernadette.

Alastair smiled when he recognized him. "Harris."

"Alastair." He nodded. "Where's Wes?"

"On the way up, I've been informed."

Harris held out a burlap bag. Alastair faced the other way. He heard the tape rip. Bernadette held up her hand.

"Alastair?" He turned around to face her. "You'll take care of her?"

"You have to ask?" Alastair responded softly.

Harris interrupted, "Hornik, book her."

The agent placed the tape over her mouth, then covered her ruined face with a burlap bag.

The rooftop emptied, save for Alastair and Harris, who waited patiently.

They heard Wes's voice. "Have they left?"

"Where are you?" Alastair called.

"Close your eyes," Wes demanded.

Alastair let his lids drop for a second, then opened them, a bark of laughter escaping his lips.

His petite daughter gently hovered above them, her apparent boyfriend in her arms.

"You weren't supposed to look until we landed," Wes said hotly. His face flushed red when he saw his father as well.

"Nice flying." Alastair held out his hand to her, his eyes warm. "Alastair Verne."

"Nice to meet you." She smiled shyly, then looked at Harris.

"Harris Rockville." He nodded curtly. "We sort of met earlier."

"I'm the real Morgan." She looked at her father, finishing the sentence. "Apparently I'm Morgan Verne."

Alastair took her arm, resting it in the crook of his own. "We have a lot of catching up to do."

She looked at him sideways, responding, "Indeed."

Harris left them to wrap his arm around his son's shoulder. "Nice work, son. Excellent fieldwork. I'm … impressed. How did you know that creature wasn't the real Morgan?"

"My gut, sir."

Harris gave him a sideways hug, fished in his pocket, and slapped something cold into Wes's hand. "I expect to see you back in my office on Monday."

Wes looked down at the badge in his hand. It was his old one, barely used, but the one he coveted—or so he'd thought. He glanced up. The moon was three-quarters waning, a week or two away from that new moon when he'd promised to return to his old job. He held out the shield to his father, shaking his head. "Thanks, Dad. I appreciate it, but I think I'm going to stay where I am."

"I thought it would make you happy."

"I've learned that nothing can make you happy but yourself." He looked at Alastair. "I think I have a lot to learn here, and that makes me happy."

Harris grinned. "I'll tell you a secret, son. If I could change and go back, I would too. Nothing more exciting than wrestling with witches."

"Or flying."

"I know. Mom's a great flyer," Harris said with a fond chuckle, then walked briskly away.

Wes's eyes widened. "What? Dad? What did you say about Mom?" All he heard was the echoes of his father's laughter.

The street level was a mess of police and official cars. Alastair was parked on the corner. Morgan was in the back seat. Wes ran up, jumping in. "How'd you know to wait for me?" he asked.

Alastair smiled when he looked at him. "You're my partner," he said with a sheepish smile. "We have to swing by Red Hook to pick up Junie."

"Junie, right. What happened with the ships? Did the Coast Guard reach them in time?"

"Do you remember the stew she cooked?"

"I have some still glowing in my kitchen."

"Well, apparently, Junie stocked the galley with ample supplies of it."

It was two and a half miles off the coast of New York, late the previous night. Five cargo ships, their surfaces covered with stacked corrugated metal containers, bobbed gently in the Atlantic Ocean. Music blared, and someone had decorated four levels of containers with multicolored Christmas lights. Ten Coast Guard cutters surrounded the group of transports. A captain stood on the bow of the largest cutter, a bullhorn at his mouth.

"This is Luke Ross with the US Coast Guard. Who is in charge of these ships? We demand you turn around and follow us back to the Brooklyn Port."

Laughter erupted from the ship nearest the Coast Guard cutter. "Yo, *papi chulo*!" a slurred voice called. "You wanna join the party? Why don't you and all the boys come up and have some fun!" A conga line appeared from the cargo hold. A long line of inebriated sailors danced and waved to the cutters, each holding a plastic cup with a phosphorous green liquid sloshing around.

"What is that, sir?" an ensign asked Captain Ross.

"I don't know. Whatever it is, it delayed these ships long enough for us to catch them before they entered international waters."

"Ross we bring 'em in?"

Carter shrugged. "Looks like we're going to have to. Doesn't look like there's a sober sailor on any of them. Prepare to board," he called out.

"I spread the wealth." Junie chuckled good-naturedly from the back seat.

Wes made a sound.

"Look, part of my job was to ensure that all the cargo ships were full of food and water. I stock the galleys. You know, rations, to get them to their next port of call. I was nervous we weren't going to be able to stop this thing in time, so I juiced up the water supply with my stew."

"Ew," Morgan said.

"Did the trick. They was so busy drinking and partying, nobody was driving the boat," she finished with a wheezy laugh. "You're killing me here, Alastair. Can't I have a smoke in the car?"

Wes, Alastair, and Morgan all replied, "No!"

"Humor me," she wheedled.

"No," Wes said flatly.

"Then distract me with a story," Junie said coyly.

"What?" Wes asked.

"Tell me a story, you know, about what happened to you in Nevada."

Wes turned sharply in his seat. "What do you know about that?"

"I read it in your file."

"My file?"

"Yeah, here in Alastair's truck."

Alastair shrugged. "Don't ask me. She's a category five."

Morgan sat in the back, her eyes shining. "Wes, you don't have to, but I would like to know."

Wes sat sullenly for a minute, his eyes meeting Morgan's in the rearview mirror. She smiled.

"Well …" he began.

Nevada Desert, Three Months Earlier

The desert landscape resembled the moon, colorless and just as lifeless. Dust settled in every nook and cranny of the bus. They were covered with it. For a minute, they looked like soldiers in Afghanistan, in full body armor, down to protective visors painting everything a darker gray. Two men sat in the first row, assault guns in their ready hands, the stock of a twelve-gauge resting on the seat. Wes sat toward the rear, next to Simon Samuels, an ex-Marine who captained their expedition. It was a big deal to be placed with Samuels. He was a decorated legend and had taken on Wes as a favor to Harris. They were transporting a highly dangerous criminal. That was all the information Wes had.

In the rear, the prisoner rested, her blue-veined hands neatly in her lap, and hummed sweetly. Wes glanced at her legs. She wore support hose like he remembered his great-grandmother wearing, tied in a rolled knot at the top of her calf. Her feet in their open-toed thick-soled sandals tapped in rhythm to her song. Wes couldn't help the smile tugging at his lips. A burlap bag covered her head.

"Something funny, Agent Rockville?" the captain asked. His dark skin was covered in sweat, but he seemed oblivious to the discomfort Wes felt.

"What's her story?" Wes whispered.

Samuels sighed. "Didn't they teach you anything at the academy, rookie? I know your daddy is the director and all, but you have to be on your A-game here."

"Just because my dad's the director doesn't mean I can't be curious," Wes said with a smile. The two guards turned around, looking like the young men they were. The bus seemed to lose its tension for a millisecond. Wes noticed the driver was looking at them in the rearview mirror as well. It seemed he wasn't the only nosy one.

Samuels's brown eyes darted around the room. "Didn't you go over your brief?" he asked a shade harshly.

The humming got louder, as if she were trying to engage with them. Wes cocked his head—the song was so familiar. Where had he heard it?

"Yeah, I went over my brief. Three times."

The lead guard smiled at their discussion.

"And what did your brief say, Agent Rockville?"

"Don't look her in the eyes, sir." This time, Wes and the three guards grinned at one another as they exchanged looks.

"And ...?" the captain continued brusquely.

"Don't ask any questions?"

"So, don't ask any questions." The captain's mouth closed, but Wes saw the beginning of a smile.

"It's just that ..." He paused, waiting to see if the captain would close him down.

"Yes?"

"It's just that I find it weird we're transporting this little old lady with such high security. I mean, she's harmless."

"Yeah, Captain. Look at her." The guard in the front twisted in his seat, joining the conversation. "She looks like she should be baking cookies, not rotting in the back of a hot bus with her head covered. What'd she do?"

"It's inhumane," the bus driver added.

The frail voice got a little louder, the words to the song just barely audible under the burlap bag covering her head.

"Hello, ma baby! Hello, ma honey! Hello, ma ragtime gal!"

"I know this song," the driver shouted, joining in the next chorus. *"Send me a kiss by wire. Baby, my heart's on fire!"*

Wes noticed the captain's foot tapping in time to the song, his mouth moving, silently singing the lyrics. He felt the song vibrate in his chest, then the words erupted from his lips.

"If you refuse me, honey, you'll lose me; then you'll be left alone."

By now, they were all singing loudly, the bag covering Genevieve Fox's face half off her white, frizzy hair. Her cheeks were powder soft, chubby, with sweet pink undertones. Her cornflower-blue eyes peeked out. She was singing with gusto, her old-lady voice joyous. *"Oh baby, telephone and tell me I'm your own. Hello, hello, hello there!"*

They were all laughing. Wes turned around, his eyes meeting hers. She tilted her head and blew a kiss at him that impacted with terminal velocity. His eyes slipped shut and he rolled down the seat, fast asleep. The two guards in the front followed him to slumber a second later. Samuels grabbed his rifle, only to feel it slide through his fingers as he rocked forward. The driver slumped and the bus rolled into a berm, halting when Miss Fox snapped her fingers. Listing sideways, she made it down the aisle, the shackles on her feet melting away. Pausing, she caressed Wes's face. "Nice boy," she said sweetly.

Raising her manacled hands high over her head, Fox let out a sonic roar that blasted out every window, breaking the handcuffs in two. She chuckled, then rolled her hands together, creating a whirlwind of energy that blew a starburst through the roof. Taking a shotgun, Miss Fox seated herself sidesaddle and took a leisurely ride through her escape hole. Turning demurely, she called back, "So long, suckers!"

She soared out, crowing high into the ether.

Out of sight.

The End, for some, but for others, it's just the beginning ...

ACKNOWLEDGMENTS

Witches was originally self-published in 2015 and became my most top-selling book ever. Cut through the days, weeks, and years, and *Witches* has finally been published under the fabulous Kevin J. Anderson's banner WordFire Press.

I would like to express my sincere gratitude to Kevin and his team for taking the idea and putting their magical publishing spells on one of my favorite manuscripts. You are all an absolute pleasure to work with.

Thanks to my literary agent Nick Mullendore at Vertical Ink who jumped on board when I told him I have a story called *Witches Protection Program.*

Thank you to my film agent Kim Yau at Paradigm for explaining and mentoring me on why a screenplay has to be totally different from the book.

Thanks to my West Coast mom and entertainment attorney Susan Grode at Katten Muchin Rosenman for believing in the magic and teaching me to keep my mouth shut (which has been very hard to do).

I would like to say a big thank you to Sharon, Alexander,

Cayla, Eric, Jennifer, Hallie, and Zachary. A shout out to my son Alexander for helping me create some of the steampunk guns in the *Witches* universe.

Last but not least, a big thank you to my mom. You are the voice of reason and without you, my writing career would be nothing but a dream.

Last and certainly not least, a thank you to my dad, who never got to see the publishing of *Witches* in physical form, but is helping me out more than I can ever imagine from over there. Thanks Pop.

And seriously last but not least, the readers and fans. My gosh. You are the reason I write every day of my life. Without your love, support, and constructive criticism, I'd be lost on this journey. Thank you all for being a part of this incredible ride. More stories are coming, so hang on!

ABOUT THE AUTHOR

Michael Okon is the award-winning, best-selling author of fifteen books, including *Monsterland* and *Monsterland Reanimated*. Michael writes full time and lives on the North Shore of Long Island with his wife and children.

Photo by Owen Kassimir

IF YOU LIKED ...

IF YOU LIKED WITCHES PROTECTION PROGRAM, YOU
MIGHT ALSO ENJOY:

Monsterland
by Michael Okon

Monsterland Reanimated
by Michael Okon

Zomnibus
by Kevin J. Anderson

Selected Stories: Horror and Dark Fantasy
by Kevin J. Anderson